Kristin Osborne is a real estate foreclosure prevention specialist, horse lover, and single mother of her daughter, Ashley Noel Osborne and her son Ryan Tyler Osborne, who is an autistic cancer survivor and psychic medium and whose deep love of nature and historical homes brought her from her native home in Los Angeles, California to Virginia in 2010. She now resides in Gloucester, Virginia with her daughter and son and her two Belgian draft horses, Zeus and Coconut and thoroughbred Zachary and is currently writing her second non-fiction book, a sequel to *Behind the Veil.*

Behind the Veil is dedicated in the highest honor, glory, and gratitude to Jesus Christ, Archangel Michael and his Legions of Angels, Archangel Metatron, Archangel Raphael, Archangel Uriel, and Archangel Chamuel, whom cleared our home from the wrath of Satan and his demons and blessed our home and grounds with their love, light and angels, and the holiest and magical experience anyone can ever imagine in life. God guided me to pen this book in his honor and has blessed us with peace, hope, joy, and the light and love of Jesus Christ and His angels in faith.

Kristin Osborne

BEHIND THE VEIL

AUSTIN MACAULEY PUBLISHERS™
LONDON • CAMBRIDGE • NEW YORK • SHARJAH

Copyright © Kristin Osborne (2021)

All rights reserved. No part of this publication may be reproduced, distributed, or transmitted in any form or by any means, including photocopying, recording, or other electronic or mechanical methods, without the prior written permission of the publisher, except in the case of brief quotations embodied in critical reviews and certain other noncommercial uses permitted by copyright law. For permission requests, write to the publisher.

Any person who commits any unauthorized act in relation to this publication may be liable to criminal prosecution and civil claims for damages.

This is a work of fiction. Names, characters, businesses, places, events, locales, and incidents are either the products of the author's imagination or used in a fictitious manner. Any resemblance to actual persons, living or dead, or actual events is purely coincidental.

Ordering Information
Quantity sales: Special discounts are available on quantity purchases by corporations, associations, and others. For details, contact the publisher at the address below.

Publisher's Cataloging-in-Publication data
Osborne, Kristin
Behind the Veil

ISBN 9781643783826 (Paperback)
ISBN 9781643783642 (Hardback)
ISBN 9781643781938 (ePub e-book)

Library of Congress Control Number: 2021914864

www.austinmacauley.com/us

First Published (2021)
Austin Macauley Publishers LLC
40 Wall Street, 33rd Floor, Suite 3302
New York, NY 10005
USA

mail-usa@austinmacauley.com
+1 (646) 5125767

I would like to thank my daughter, Ashley Noel Osborne, and my son, Ryan Tyler Osborne, for their encouragement, support, and unconditional love in my life and my father, Lon Klein of Haleiwa Surfboard Co., who taught me to live passionately, shoot for the stars, and to never give up, my mother Sharon Klein and my brother Erich Klein for always encouraging me to be self-employed in the mortgage industry so I could work at home with my children and horses after my divorce and to Stewart for purchasing Eagle Point Plantation on Valentine's Day of 2016 and making my dreams come true.

And thank you to Austin Macauley publishers for your encouragement and outstanding professionalism in my endeavors.

Behind the Veil is a true story about a fairytale romance with my narcissistic boyfriend Stewart, my son Ryan who is an autistic, psychic medium and a cancer survivor and our experience living in a haunted abandoned pre-Civil War slave plantation possesed by the devil in Gloucester, Virginia by Kristin Osborne.

Kristin is a tall blonde-haired, blue-eyed single parent of Ashley Noel, a Christmas day baby, and extremely bright; and Ryan, an autistic, psychic, medium with a speech impairment.

I am a Manhattan Beach, California native and an ex professional hunter show rider that I gave up my career in sales at Warner Bros for; loves nature, gardening, and cooking and has had a history of prophecy and the spirit world and finding haunted houses and is from lineage of Robert E. Lee.

In reflection almost every single house I have lived in had ghosts and spirits in it. I was a speed reader from the age of five and preferred books like Nostradamus and Jung and the first time I read the Bible I was so terrified I couldn't finish it.

Interestingly enough my mother went to an all catholic girls school with Lana Turner and she never once in my childhood took me to church, we never said grace, my parents never talked about God nor did we ever have a cross symbol in our home.

My father was a very successful contractor that built custom homes, we moved constantly. My mother was a stay at home artist and made yarn from sheep's wool and made weavings and pottery.

I had a fairytale childhood growing up at art fairs, sand castle contests, beach volleyball, horse showing and taking every elective class at the community center, ballet, drama, guitar, gymnastics you name it.

Unfortunately when I was nine my parents got divorced, my dad moved to northern California with his new wife and my mother went to work full time as a paralegal.

I was absolutely crushed over my parents divorce, lost all of any self-confidence I had and ended up being a latchkey child and spent every second of my life at the stables, my father bought me a horse probably out of guilt.

After I graduated high school, I landed a job at Universal Pictures in feature business affairs and then transferred to Warner Bros.

I met my first husband at a horse show, fell in love, got married and quit my job at Warner Bros to horse show full time and then got the maternal itch at age 30 and got pregnant and we moved to his family farm in San Diego.

I found a vacant race horse farm that we bought while I was pregnant and I built a home and we had Ashley Noel my first child on Christmas day. I loved being a mother and loved my life.

I got pregnant again and then had Ryan Tyler. Fatherhood ended up being too much for my ex, our marriage lasted four years and then he disappeared leaving me with two toddlers and seven horses.

I managed to get my life in order, sold our home, gave most of the horses away and moved back to Los Angeles where my mom and brother lived.

My brother is an extremely successful bank executive and helped me get started in the mortgage industry selling pay option arms so I could stay home with my kids.

In 2010, I was working at home as a loan officer and had made a considerable amount of money saving people's homes from foreclosure in the real estate market crash and had established a very strong network of consistent referrals from clients for several years. At that time, I had five horses in my backyard, Zeus and Coconut my blonde Belgian draft horses I rescued from a Premarin farm in South Dakota, Zachary an ex racehorse from Texas and two other young thoroughbreds I had bought for resale from Santa Anita Racetrack.

My daughter Ashley was struggling with bullies at school, she went to the nurses' office almost every day sick so she could come home and Ryan was having behavioral problems due to not being able to speak.

I was leasing an adorable Cape Cod style home with a six stall barn near the Los Angeles National forest at the time and my house bills were averaging ten thousand dollars a month, a bale of hay was currently over thirty dollars and gasoline was five dollars a gallon.

I remember the first night I moved into that house, it had been empty for some time, my kids and I went grocery shopping to stalk up the refrigerator and an elderly male ghost walked into the kitchen and picked up all the groceries I had set on the counter and threw them all over the place and then walked straight through the brick wall and disappeared and never came back. This didn't phase me in the least.

I was working fourteen hours a day seven days a week and my only social life was with a pagan group network that satisfied my insatiable thirst for knowledge about ghosts, the spirit world and magic, most all of whom lived on the East Coast. For some reason I developed a deep fascination for the Greek deities.

I had a vision to move to the east coast and I would meet the man of my dreams and live happily ever after.

I decided on either North Carolina or Virginia and started house shopping and I decided on purchasing a single-story brick ranch house with five acres and a stable in Gladys, Virginia and shipped my five horses and drove my kids across country to my family's new home. Arriving in Virginia was like arriving in a history book filled with Civil War memorabilia and churches everywhere.

Our first night here we were blessed with a shooting star and a double rainbow and the start of our new life's journey that would reunite my family with faith in God and Jesus Christ and his angels.

Shortly after settling in Ryan was diagnosed with Ewing's sarcoma cancer. He had a tumor behind his left ear and had to have an emergency surgery and was diagnosed with a 30% survival rate. Ryan would have to endure nine months of inpatient chemotherapy, thirty days of radiation and three blood transfusions.

It took a while for this to sink in to me, I refused to accept the doctor's diagnosis that Ryan may not survive and forged ahead with blinders on to keep my business afloat, I had put a huge down payment on the house I just bought and had five horses to support in addition to my children.

I stayed with Ryan in his hospital room alternating three and five days per and took my computer and printer and worked on my loan files and my referral network to make as much money as I could. This ended up being the only way to keep my sanity to survive the next nine months of Ryan's cancer treatment.

I had to give Ryan Neupogen injections at home every day he wasn't hospitalized and also to a different hospital for lab work.

I had to hire neighbors to take care of the horses and the Williams family from the Ebinezer Baptist Church who lived across the street from me offered to take care Ashley whilst I was gone so she could stay in school.

At the same time one of my neighbors introduced me to a man named Stewart who was a real estate investor and also self-employed. Stewart was 18 years older than I and was divorced twice and lived up the street from me in a huge Georgian Plantation on 800 acres and the Staunton river on what used to be a slave plantation. I completely blew Stewart off the first few times he came by to visit me.

Stewart happened to owned almost the entire town of Brookneal; a small depressed town in a semi-rural area next to Gladys. He had lived there for almost thirty years and everyone in town knew him. I kept turning him away and he wouldn't give up.

A few months into Ryan's cancer treatment who by the way never complained even once, I was feeling vulnerable and needed a distraction from the reality of my kids' situation I called Stewart one day out of the blue and asked him over for dinner.

Stewart and I had instant sexual chemistry after the first time we hugged. I ended up falling hopelessly in love with him. I should have listened to his friends that said the only thing he cared about is sex and food.

Stewart had an insatiable sexual appetite and preferred that I cooked him three gourmet meals a day. He said he had to take one night off to stay at home since he insisted on sleeping with me every night. I would sadly find out why later on.

I was happily in love and after Stewart took me on a tour of his forty rental houses that were mostly empty, I decided he needed my help.

Ryan had been successfully discharged from his cancer treatment and both my children were getting attached to Stewart.

I devoted my life to cleaning and renting Stewart's rentals, I did all of his advertising, maintenance work and paperwork and picked up his rents for him.

I decided to take a break from my own loan business, I was burnt out and the Make a Wish Foundation granted Ryan a twelve-day vacation to Orlando, Florida and I took Stewart with me thinking we were going to get married.

Stewart and I ended up taking Lynchburg by storm, we cashed out his stock and bought a historical library in Lynchburg and I did a rezoning for him to turn it into an event center and I was interviewed by the local television stations and on tv and in the news almost every day.

Using my loan officer skills, I negotiated several other short sales on historical mansions in downtown Lynchburg that he purchased for pennies on the dollar.

I was so enamored by Stewart I didn't realize what I was doing, I wasn't going to ever benefit financially for all the money I was making him.

Stewart talked me into moving to his farm to an empty huge four bedroom home he had on the other side of his property and I agreed since we spent all of our time together and my horses would have 800 acres to graze on and my kids and I could swim in the river right in front of our house.

We dated for five years in a whirlwind romance and we went on vacation to Chesapeake Bay one weekend and decided to go look at a few plantations I had found for sale and Eagle Point Plantation and I found each other. Old, empty, haunted houses always have a way of finding me.

Stewart loves to buy real estate and we both fell in love with Eagle Point. He said he wanted to retire there and sell his rental houses and thought it was perfect for me with the horse set up and indoor riding arena.

It took us two years to negotiate a contract to purchase Eagle Point Plantation and at the same time we negotiated a contract with an investment company to purchase

Stewart's real estate portfolio. Unfortunately for Stewart the sale of his rentals fell through a week after he bought Eagle Point and I was going to move to Eagle Point by myself with my kids to rent the tenant homes and get the house in order.

The plantation had been emptied for over 12 years. The main house was originally built in 1680, and was occupied by Jonathan Bryant, a member of the King's Council in Richmond and who was instrumental in the Civil War and freeing religion in Virginia.

Eagle Point is adjacent to the famous Warner Hall Plantation which was originally occupied by Queen Elizabeth II. Eagle Point was abandoned in the Yankee invasion and the soldiers fled by boat to Yorktown. The plantation was then ransacked by carpetbaggers and Blackbeard pirates who traded with the Powhatan Indians, Norse, French and British at the cove in front of the plantation on the Severn River.

Eagle Point traded hands many times; all occupants ended up fleeing the house shortly after purchasing it or died at an early age in the home. The O'Grady family bought the plantation in 1905 and added the east wing and Georgian columns on the front porch, with lots of Greek architecture and depictions of cupid; they must have been pagans. They abandoned the house and it was empty until 1950, when a French family bought it as a weekend home and named it *C'est la Rue*, or Water Street. They built a pool, pool house, horse stables and three guest homes and a hunting shack. Their family died at a young age and a

Japanese real estate developer bought Eagle Point; he went bankrupt and never lived in the home. The plantation sat empty until 1990, when the Carruthers family purchased it. He added timber, cropland more stables and a workshop. The Carruthers stayed in the apartment above the barn instead of the home and the Carruthers had a heart attack at his desk the day the stock market crashed. Eagle Point reverted to Carruthers estate and sat empty until Stewart purchased the farm.

Kristin, Ashley and Ryan moved to Eagle Point, May 22nd of 2016. We decorated all 12 bedrooms with old antiques and Persian rugs from one of Stewart's airplane hangers and settled right in with our three horses, Zeus, Coconut and Zachary; our two cats Daphne and Eva; and 20 India blue and white peacocks. We were in awe over the water view watching the boats, blue herons, egrets, storks, eagles, falcons, ospreys, hawks, cardinals, Canadian geese and blue jays.

Little did we know what we were in store for here; the most spiritually enlightening experience anyone could ever imagine restoring faith in God, conquering fear and incredible visits from Jesus Christ, Archangel Michael and his legions of angels, Archangel Metatron and Almighty God himself; battling demons, Satan and marching thousands of Civil War soldiers and servant ghosts of the plantation up a staircase to heaven and restoring peace, joy, and harmony to God's land here at Eagle Point Plantation.

I have since I was a young girl always experienced prophecy, telepathy, clairsentience, clairaudience and to be able to see ghosts. Ryan, being an empath, did not open up until winter of 2017 that he is a psychic medium and visits with God and Jesus Christ quite often. This was confirmed by a professional, certified angelic psychic medium I took Ryan to; although I had no doubt in my mind that he was honest when he told me later on that God took him to heaven with Jesus Christ, while he was in the hospital during his emergency ear surgery and it was the 30 days of radiation aimed at his pineal gland that magnified his third eye, or crown chakra, and miraculously opened up his vocabulary as he was nonverbal until we move to Virginia.

The first year, we settled right in. Stewart stayed in Lynchburg to manage his real estate portfolio so we didn't get to see him very often; another twist in divine timing to rediscover myself, my spirituality and pay more attention to Ryan's needs. This will make more sense to you later on.

Ashley went to California to visit her grandmother, and then to Hawaii to visit her grandfather and decided to go to college in Richmond for convenience so Ryan and I had a whopping 12000 square foot plantation all to ourselves.

Interestingly, I felt nothing but peace here in this home that never made any noise except the singing stairs that sing in the wind storms. I experienced a lot of sadness with my daughter leaving but came to terms for what was best for her, and a lot of it was because she did not want to be around Stewart.

Ryan started flourishing in school. I started a horse boarding business and enjoyed riding my own horses in my indoor arena and on the trails. Ryan and I had so much fun exploring the attic and the basement—which has a walk-in safe used during the Civil War and has elaborate catacombs of rooms which were servant's quarters, and Roman-style basins to trap water from storms for the servants to carry water up the staircases to their masters.

Stewart bought an RTV with four-wheel drive, we had so much fun exploring around the coves, picking wild blackberries and collecting oyster shells for the garden.

Ryan and I survived our first tropical storm and a mandatory hurricane evacuation which we did not have the means to evacuate, several power outages and a freezing winter with no heater.

On our first Christmas, we cut a of 15-foot cedar tree from the yard for the dining room and had a beautiful Christmas.

I leased all of the guest cottages, the apartment above the stable and took on more horse boarders and gave riding lessons and started making friends in the community and settling in.

I didn't realize at that time that Stewart was to become a non-existent part of my life due to his business and the time I'm spending alone gives me more time to realize his narcissistic tendencies. It was a slow process; what I thought was the one true love of my life, replaced by divine love, guidance and a return to my soul by Jesus Christ and his magical angels.

I learned shortly thereafter to not be on a too friendly basis with tenants. After managing Stewart's 50 rental house portfolio for 5 years, it was worse when in your own farm, it only takes one person to rock the boat and caused dissension.

One of the tenants on the property that lived in the guest cottage next to my kitchen for no reason became insanely jealous of me and trifling disrespectful and I would find out later why after I was taught by Christ how the devil leads you into temptation with horrible emotions like jealousy, anger and fear.

She was jealous that I was attractive and in a relationship with a handsome wealthy man, she wanted to be in my shoes. If she only knew the truth about the challenges of pleasing a narcissist, she probably would have changed her mind.

We were visited quite frequently by unwelcome psychic and ghost hunters and relatives of the Civil War soldiers, all that claimed Eagle Point was the most haunted plantation in Virginia and full of ghosts. I never let any of them in the house and I couldn't see a ghost anywhere. I felt nothing but peace here.

Another tenant in one of the rental houses claimed to be a medium, along with her horribly rude daughter, and told me there were thousands of ghosts in front of my house and yard all over the place. I just ignored her. She ended at being a huge troublemaker that we ended up evicting; one of the demons must have left with her as she became vengeful against me. When it comes to mediumship and the spiritual world, whatever you do comes back to you tenfold.

Ever since I was a little girl, my motto was harm none, and to this day, and I am still a vegetarian and would not hurt anyone.

Ryan and I spent a lot of time outside that summer; we fell in love with the nature here and would take hundreds of pictures of the house, the grounds and the peacocks and promoting the horse business.

Ryan was appreciating having more time from mom as he was growing up into a young man and the growing friction from Stewart and my relationship greatly affected him.

Stewart and I started having some pretty nasty fights, little did I know all was from the spirits that lived in the house and what was to come in the future. Stewart was not happy that I was no longer at his disposal and we both didn't realize how much work it was going to be just to maintain the grounds.

I poured my heart and soul into the house and land trying to maintain a 12000 square foot house; take care of the nine horses I have boarded; my autistic son, and my demanding boyfriend that loved to upset me terribly; and mowing hundred acres gras. I started to lose weight and get exhausted and irritable and thought I was going to have a stroke.

I didn't pay much attention to why all the flowers I planted died when I have a natural green thumb.

Charlie Carruthers ghost came in my kitchen to introduce himself to me one morning, don't ask me how I knew who he was I just did. He said he wanted to see who was living in his plantation, he truly loved this place and then he got furious that I was living here alone with my children and was mortified that Stewart was not taking care of the farm to his standards.

I just smiled at him and he disappeared through the kitchen wall and never returned.

I started obsessing, taking pictures and videos of the spirits in the house and the nature spirits in the sky and the things out of the window of my second-floor office, which looks out on the driveway and above the dock that washed away in hurricane Katrina.

I was frustrated that the spirits weren't talking to me, what were the alien things in the sky and not one ghost showed up in my pictures.

Near Thanksgiving are second one in the home, I started feeling an almost suffocating tension in the house. I would play Celtic music for hours and laugh as the doors in the stable would swing open when I neared the barn and close by themselves for me. I laughed it was probably a fairy. The Plantation was so quiet you could hear a pin drop, and quite frequently I would hear footsteps running up and down the stairs, doors and windows upstairs opening and closing and whispers of sounded like children crying or screaming.

I didn't think much of it, for some reason the only thing that bothered me was what sounded like an extremely loud growling howling noise that came from the sky above the house when there was no wind and the front and side door bell chimes going off in the middle of the night when there was no one outside.

We found a used furnace for a portion of the house and I decided to decorate for Christmas the weekend after Thanksgiving. I asked a neighbor to cut a cedar tree for me and put the tree in the dining room, it was huge, beautiful and I spent days decorating it with hundreds of Christmas balls.

The dining room is my favorite place to entertain, if only the walls could speak. Queen Elizabeth II, Lord Baltimore, Robert E. Lee and other generals used to have ballroom dances in there.

I found a really neat pre-Civil War cast iron cooking pot from the storage barn that I put in my stable with some antiques. Later on, I will learn it was a cauldron used by one of the servants that practiced black magic here.

I became obsessed with the history of Eagle Point from thousands of years ago. One day, I came back to the house after taking care of the horses and I couldn't find my obese cat Daphne.

I walked all over the house calling for her and could hear from meowing but could not find her.

I went upstairs to my daughter's wing and kept calling her but couldn't find her. A little voice in my head told me to check the attic. I opened the door to the attic and she was on top of the stairs with a wild look in her green eyes. I carried her downstairs. No one else was on the grounds or the home.

I have good intuition and can normally smell the scent of another person that would enter my home. This one had me stumped. I went about my day.

And at about the same time, I noticed my son started acting strange only wanting to hide in his room play acting with his imaginary friends, you could hear him and other children talking, laughing and playing with his toys and running around his room. I would go upstairs and there would be no else but Ryan.

I rationalized this to myself as clairaudience, sometimes I can hear conversations from miles away.

That night, after dinner, I walked through the dining room to go to my bedroom and the Christmas tree balls were flying around in the air and rolling on the floor like bowling balls and the Christmas balls were rolling up and down the hallway to the east wing, the hallway here reminds me of the house they filmed the Shining in.

The first thought that came to me was there was a poltergeist here. Not a very relaxing night. I decided to go upstairs to the east wing second floor to turn some lights on and a voice called out to me 'hello Kristin, you are now the lady of the house, my name is Lorna Bryant.'

I turned around and my spine shivered, there was a beautiful brunette dainty ghost dressed in a white Victorian style floor length dress with a gorgeous wide brimmed Victorian hat, she wore a corset and high lace up boots and was very elegant.

I was wearing a strapless dress with flip flops, I must have looked ridiculous to her. Lorna then said, 'Kristin why don't you grow up and start acting like a lady and tell that horrid man Stewart to repair the home.'

For some reason I started laughing so hard I almost cried and then she went into the other room and sat down on an antique gold French fainting couch I had put in there and I went back downstairs and wrote her name down.

It turned out after I researched her name that she had died in the house from the flu and was the daughter of

Jonathan Bryant and was buried at the Pine Island graveyard next to the house.

I kept hearing footsteps like a whole bunch of people walking and banging around Ryan's room which is above my bedroom and footsteps and doors slamming all around the house.

The next morning, after I took Ryan to the school bus and turned out the horses and made a cup of coffee and went to sit in bed and pet my cats while I drank my coffee—my son's bathroom is directly above my bathroom and his bedroom is above my bedroom—I heard clawing on his bathroom walls like a lion or a demon scratching, banging on the floor for about an hour. The clawing noise was absolutely hideous and I also heard the horrible loud growling hissing sound just like the one that would come from above the house.

My cats were terrified and hid under the bed. It took all of nerves to force myself to go upstairs to Ryan's room in case someone had broken in. I took my cellphone in case I needed to call 911. My heart was beating a million a second I was afraid. Fear is the most suffocating horrible thing to feel, I was also completely defenseless.

There was no one there. I took a picture, sometimes things show up in pictures that the human eye can't see and my phone popped off with an explosion and went dead the second I went to take a picture.

I literally ran back downstairs to recharge my phone and had the most suffocating feeling creppy everywhere in the house except for in my bedroom.

I forced myself to calm down and make breakfast and go on a walk to the barn and that was last day I would have cell phone service inside my house; but I could still take pictures.

And that was the day the house became alive. Unexplainable things started to happen. Ryan would walk the hallways with a bizarre grin on a face and he would avoid me completely.

I asked him if he had ghost friends and his room he was talking to and he replied there were no such things as ghosts. Every morning, the same routine with that horrible clawing, growling hideous scratching noise on the walls in Ryan's room and the banging in his bathroom.

It sounded like an army marching around the house, the lights would go on and off, the doors would swing open and closed and I could hear voices crying, screaming or laughing.

I became more obsessed taking pictures everywhere trying to understand the things that showed up. I also had a bad habit of taking nude selfies to entertain Stewart when he wasn't here in front of my eight-foot by ten-foot gold brides dressing mirror in the foyer, and one day I heard a voice call me, "Kristin stop photographing yourself you are so vain and un lady like." I thought to myself so the mirror speaks, very interesting.

Later on, I would learn this was the voice of Elizabeth O'Grady who died at Eagle Point in the early 1900s, whose spirit lives here in the library room on the first floor and does not like my decorating, and despises Stewart for not repairing the house.

Every single night the Christmas balls would fly and roll around the house and Ryan would walk up and down the hallway with the most bizarre grin on his face and he seemed to be completely unaware of my presence.

I would blast Celtic music, go ride my horses for hours and then dance until I fell asleep from sheer exhaustion, not knowing what I was going to see or hear next in the house and my fear was getting out of control.

I would go to my daughter's bathroom second floor bathroom underneath the attic to bathe at night as fast as I could I didn't feel safe up there and then try to go to bed.

One night after I took a long hot bubble bath, I went to walk down the three flights of stairs to go to my bedroom which was originally the men's cigar smoking room and I felt a tall man breath down my neck and he tried to put his arms around me. I grabbed the handrail of the staircase and literally ran back to my room and heard him running behind me.

I turned around to see if he was real or a ghost, he was about six feet tall and had blonde hair and blue eyes and wore a soldier's uniform. I said leave me alone and slammed the door in the ghost's face and locked it. My heart was racing.

Several weeks later when Stewart and I were asleep in the middle of the night I'm sure it was the same ghost that tried to climb on top of me and he was naked, I woke up out of a very deep sleep and shoved him off of me and put Stewart's arm around me and went back to sleep.

After several weeks of this, I decided I needed help; sage incense house cleansing rituals were not going to do the trick.

I made dozens of phone calls and emails to Edgar Cayse Foundation and people who referred me to someone who specialized in poltergeists—ghost hunter groups that wanted to come and record things in the house told me to keep a journal—and a shaman that said he would come and do a drum clearance in the house.

My son was acting so bizarre although he was always smiling and sympathetic to my complaints about the noise in his room and where did the claw marks come from on his mattress like someone took a razor blade too. I started making him sit in the bathroom with me while I bathed. I almost just couldn't be in my kitchen anymore unless Stewart was there, which was hardly ever.

One night, I sat on my kitchen porch with a glass of wine which faces the sunset house, a two-story rental of mine. I was looking at the sunroom door and a huge, bright white flashed out of the window of the sunset house that almost blinded me. I texted my tenant if he was using a camera flash taking pictures of me and he responded that he wasn't at home, there was no one there.

I was so upset about what was happening to my beautiful, peaceful mansion. I learned later on that the flash from the sunset house was a black magic spell from one of the servant ghosts that was abused here. The house became so suffocating I almost couldn't stand to go inside, I was almost always home alone.

My cats refused to come out from under my bed and my normally docile Belgian draft horses started snorting and spooking at nothing.

I spent hours every day sitting in my car in front of the house writing emails to every ghost hunter and spirit groups I thought would help me, I started to get to afraid to even go in the house until Ryan got home from school and anytime I tried to make a phone call inside my cellphone service would get dropped.

Finally, I got a response from a teacher at the Psychic Institute of New Jersey that was going to refer me to one of her students; an angelic spirit releaser and psychic medium.

I got a call from her later that day. Her name was Maryanne. I explained to her what was going on in the house—my cat being locked in the attic, the clawing in my son's room, the Christmas balls flying around—and she immediately picked up on my fear.

She explained to me that she channels her mediumship and works with the angelic realm and what her fees were. We clicked instantly. She asked me to take some pictures for her and she would get back to me and so I did.

The next day when she called me, I drove down the driveway away from the house to talk to her. She explained to me that there was an evil, young male ghost, a demon in Ryan's bathroom along with 6 small children ghost and a mother and daughter ghost hiding under his antique claw bathtub.

Well, I laughed; at least I wasn't crazy. We talked for a long time, she already knew everything about me and told me she went to school in London, she was a mother too and also rescued horses.

I could tell she was very concerned and she said yes there were thousands of ghosts everywhere here, and hexes and chords from the servants that practiced black magic all over the farm.

She advised me that it was going to take a long time to cleanse this huge house; I did exactly as she instructed and we established mental telepathy together. I knew her aura field was fuchsia with gold flecks, and she gave me an overwhelming feeling of love when she channeled here. She would also leave crystals all around the house and the stables.

She told me she was going to go back to Ryan's room in a few days and that she would get back to me.

This was the start of the most spiritual, magical experience anyone could ever imagine and also a test of faith and courage. I felt a huge sigh of relief over my new friendship with Maryanne.

Even though I still made Ryan sit in my bathroom while I bathed, I forced myself to cook, and spent most of my time in the stables.

A few days later, when I woke up, I felt her aura field in my room, from Maryanne, and I knew she had been here.

She called me later and told me that she was in Ryan's bathroom that morning and had called upon Archangel Michael and had released the mother and daughter ghost. She told me their names and the stories of their past life and she also released the six children ghosts Ryan had made friends with.

Evidently, Ryan's wing upstairs was originally a school house in 1680. Maryanne asked me to buy some patchouli sticks and open Ryan's windows; the next week she was going to come back to his room to expel the demon.

Ryan was not happy when he got home to find that his ghost friends upstairs were not here but he just kept bouncing on his bed and walking up and down the walls with this huge grin on his face.

One day, the next week, the horrible clawing stopped in the morning while I was drinking coffee with my cats in my bedroom. I knew Maryanne had been here, I felt a little more peace in here and there was a fuchsia and gold sunrise that morning. Maryanne called me later that day, exhausted, and told me she had to call upon Jesus Christ himself to expel the demon and that she forgot to put her hand in a bowl of salt water while she was channeling here and the demon followed her home and she had to cleanse her own home.

She asked me to cover Ryan with a blue blanket every night and put an Archangel Michael symbol in his room. She advised me to not listen to Celtic music in this home or to meditate to the Greek deities and that I would understand why later on. She advised me that it is all about love and light. I told her okay and she said she would call me in a few days.

Ryan and I spent hours cleaning his room that night it still did not feel right. The ghosts were trying to make us leave. They would follow you everywhere, breathe down your neck, trip you, turn the heater up to 80, turn the electrical panel off, and run up and down the hallways; you could hear them. All hell was breaking loose in the house.

Maryanne became my lifeline to the world and she and I spent hours talking about the history of Eagle Point, the vibration of the land and the spirits here. She was one of those human angels that come into your life as a gift from heaven, and this would be the most beautiful experience for her as she would be called to meetings with Archangel Michael every Friday night.

I tried to get some moral support and money from Stewart. He said psychics are crazy and to just ignore the ghosts. This very much hurt my feelings and I was on my own.

Maryanne called the next day, she knew the conversation Stewart and I had, of course she could read my mind. I told her I would make payments to her and send her gift cards and flowers. She had channeled to the house that morning and shared with me the stories of some of the ghosts she had released; we bonded further and laughed.

I had a rough afternoon and evening not knowing what to expect going home to the house after riding the horses; it was late dark and dreary when I walked back to the kitchen entrance I looked above the dormer and Archangel Michael showed himself to me and was standing above the kitchen dormer appearing 50-foot tall with his sword in his hand and as real as could be. I just stared in awe. Then he disappeared.

This did make me feel better. The stress was getting to me. I would find later, my conversations with the deity's had misdirected my real faith, as my name being Kristin, I was a follower of Jesus Christ as if I had been asleep for thousands of years. I am writing this book in April, 2019.

The next day, I was cleaning the indoor arena and saw an Indian chief on a white horse ghost gallop in front of me and my horses in the pasture; my horses saw it too and ran into the indoor arena snorting and prancing.

I thought, *This is fun!* Maryanne called me later that day and I shared my story with her, she tried to explain to me how long it was going to take her to cleanse the house, let alone the 400-acres, stables and other guest cottages. She asked me to text her a picture of the front of my house, which I did.

That night, after riding my horses I walked back home and looked up above the kitchen and there stood Jesus Christ himself, standing on my kitchen dormer; white wings and robes emanating divine white light, radiating love and protection. My jaw just dropped. I just stared, then he disappeared and I just cried; it did not sink in quite yet what this meant and what was going to happen. I just saw Jesus Christ. I felt so ashamed why did I not kneel, I didn't know hardly anything about Christianity.

Something that night changed me, pure inner warrior strength, integrity, honesty. My clairaudience went into the bionic man mode, my wits were to be on call every second. Jesus Christ and Archangel Michael had taken over the Plantation to battle with Satan and his demons who are sneaky, cunning and latch on to anyone who is not a follower of Christ.

The inner voice called intuition and my guardian angel were to guide me, the vision of Archangel Michael and Jesus Christ were to change my life forever and renew my relationship with God, the Holy Spirit and my son Ryan. And as God's will Stewart would slowly be completely removed from my life.

Several days went by and when I went riding in the afternoon, finally, the weather was warming up and I walked back to the house not knowing what I was going to see or hear there. I looked in front of the house and I saw a white staircase reaching from in front of the main entrance of the Plantation for miles up to heaven, with huge white clouds in the sky beyond the island at the end of the airplane runway behind the house.

Okay this is starting to sink in I thought. I've never experienced living in omnipresence and divine timing and harmony before, and don't remember ever experiencing the pure holiness of the Lord.

Living with Archangel vibration was an adjustment; their dimension is of a different audio range. At times Archangel Michael would speak to me out of nowhere or would send a message to my guides to tell me or implant a thought in my mind. I have many recordings of the angelic realm, the most beautiful sound you have ever heard in your life.

Will it ever sink in I am living in heaven on Earth at Eagle Point Plantation with Saint Michael and legions of angels. I will smile every day for the rest of my life when I remember Jesus Christ spoke to me at 3:33am and said "Kristin, come follow me."

The next day, I was guided to a window to the right of the front foyer and took a few pictures which revealed an angel portal to heaven right in front of the house.

The pictures of this from my office that faces the main driveway showed beautiful angels all up and down the driveway.

Maryanne's presence around the farm was like an instant happy frequency, she always left crystals all around the house and barn and her love. I loved her soothing voice. She called me the next day and told me she had channeled with the Powhatan Indian chief who told her he did not want white people in this land, as we kill all the coyotes, deer, and crabs.

I told her about the staircase to heaven; I saw she grew increasingly worried about me and told me to stay away from a cave if I saw one. She then told me she was called to a meeting with Archangel Michael and the angelic realm that Friday; I told her that I had seen Jesus Christ and Archangel Michael several days ago here and she replied, "you actually saw Jesus Christ and Archangel Michael?" and I replied yes. She sounded very concerned about me and told me how special it was for her to be called to meetings with Archangel Michael.

She told me she had released a servant ghost that day from my kitchen by the name of Polly, I researched her lineage, and her family is buried here on the Pine Island graveyard.

Polly was very fond of me Maryanne said and then told me that there was a negative entity under the land, some deep seeded root to Satan wondered why I wanted to stay here. I kept sending her more pictures. I was guided to places by the angels to take pictures to send to her.

There was a dragon spirit in my backyard and other nature spirits in the front yard and beautiful angels showed up in my pictures and I could hear my guardian angel talk to Archangel Michael at times.

Doing research on the cove, I found that Latitude 37 or the Extraterrestrial Highway runs straight above my cove by the pool. I shared this with Maryanne. She was not fond of aliens. She became worried that I was going to be abducted.

During that week, she worked more on Ryan and told me that he had an incubus and two succubi attached to him which were demonic. And that's what the claw marks were on his mattress. She also removed an alien tentacle behind his left ear where the cancer sarcoma was removed and cleansed his body of the chemotherapy drugs that were still in his system six years later.

She told me he had dozens of ethereal attachments from his hospitalization, and I had more ethereal attachments she had ever seen in her life and that I suffered from terrible abandonment issues.

She told me I had been reincarnated many times. We became very close friends and we agreed that we knew each other and were followers of Jesus Christ in our past life.

The next Friday, I noticed there were many, many more angels stationed all over the property around the home and around the angel portal.

Maryanne called me again and told me that she was asked to another meeting with Archangel Michael that night in the angelic realm; I could feel their vibration presence in the house as if in heaven.

That night, when I came back to the house after riding, the entire plantation was completely covered with grids of brilliant indigo blue and crystal white dazzling lay lines and what appeared to be like a glistening diamond like shield covering the home, these were the works of Archangel Michael and Christ. Absolutely beautiful divine love, completely enamored I stared for hours.

The next morning Maryanne called me and told me that she and Archangel Michael and his legions of angels had marched thousands of Civil War soldiers up that staircase to heaven in front of my house, as well as dozens of servant ghosts. It was almost as if the house cried to have all of those ghosts released. Even the nature spirits cried in joy.

Maryanne was exhausted and drained but was ecstatic being called to the meeting with the angelic realm.

Angels are so much fun and magical; they would do things like put 7 blue herons on my back-porch railing, bring schools of thousands of blackbirds swirling above the farm and Archangel Uriel would appear in the sky, thousands of ospreys swirling above the house and leave angel feathers and coins all over the house. This would bless me for the rest of my life.

The next day, I went to the stables to feed my horses and I just sobbed with a sigh of relief over what I just went through and who could I share this with other than a psychic medium or an angel, the whole experience was starting to sink in.

And that was when Jesus Christ, dressed just as he was before he was crucified, sat down next to me in the barn on the bench next to Zeus stall as real as anyone. Was my brain able to process this, I am sitting next to God. I have never felt such a pure holy, unconditionally divine pure love feeling I could ever imagine beyond my wildest imagination.

My conversations with Jesus Christ lasted for several days; he spent two days with me here in my stable and told me I was going to really have to sacrifice myself for Ryan, meaning in a way that my integral calling in life was to be his mother first and that I was to put being of integral service to my children at the utmost importance at times. I would be reminded of this quite frequently over the years.

I would find later on that Ryan is a reincarnated angel himself; a descendant of Paul the Apostle, and has a very important role in the future of Jesus Christ's second coming. In the future I will always smile when I go to mass and realize how blessed Ryan and I.

And this was the beginning of peeling layers of vibration of the land and the spirit world. It took me a few weeks to recover my strength and I was immensely enjoying the peace and divine harmony and joy at Eagle Point.

Maryanne and I had formed mental telepathy together and she had left her cords all around the house and stables. One morning, I was having coffee in my bed, petting my cats, and I heard what sounded like something the size of a dragon land upon a dormer above my bedroom. I immediately texted Maryanne, who responded right back.

That night she called me and said yes, she had released the dragon; the dragon was real and a rainbow of colors. She said the dragon was so beautiful, she cried. I'm thinking, *Wow, this is fun!*

The legend reveals that the Norse who used to sail here to trade with the pirates and the Indians had to have a dragon aboard their ship, as an offering of peace, to enter the cove here.

One of the pictures I took of the cove shows a pirate ship above the cove that had sunk here; the Archangel Michael told me it was full of gold bullion and that was where the dragon came from.

Eagle Point is such a magical place, fairytale land. we are so blessed with divine violet sunrises, beautiful nature spirits and holy birds.

You can always tell when Jesus Christ and the Archangels come here. You can hear their presence land on the kitchen dormer and the angels sing and play the trumpet and thousands of ospreys will be swirling above the house that will disappear into thin air; they also leave angel feathers in the house.

It will take a while with my readings of the scriptures and some special photographs I took to learn that a "veil" is a holy place such as a tabernacle and God has a "veil" right above my house and a tabernacle in the attic.

About a week later, while I was having my morning coffee again, I heard something of a massive size land on my bedroom dormer. My intuition guessed it was a gigantic serpent. I could hear it slowly slithering above the house. This was an evil one I immediately sensed. I texted Maryanne. Later that day, she called me and she told me she had channeled to the house. She said it was a gigantic snake with strange tendrils on its head and she released it. I had felt her fuchsia and gold Aura field in my bedroom. She said she threw as many crystals as she could around the house.

We talked for a while. She told me I needed to put a pyramid around myself of protection when I walked the grounds or rode my horse, and a circle of protection 10-foot wide around myself and Ryan when Stewart was here, as he was the epitome of a slave plantation owner and tended to bring ghosts from his own slave plantation he lives at in Gladys, to Eagle Point, as well as negative energy.

Maryanne told me this land had so many vibrations from thousands of years; she tried to be comforting but I could tell she was tired and this would be a never-ending story.

We kept in touch and she finally told me she felt very uncomfortable channeling here anymore, as she had fear of being abducted by the extraterrestrials that have colonized here. She told me she had shared some of the pictures I had sent her with a psychic friend that specializes in aliens and that the spirits like appeared with four light forms were aliens.

I told her I understood, she had gone beyond the call of duty with her time and energy for me. Before she hung up the phone call, I heard her whisper to her daughter, 'Kristin is going into training with the Lord.'

Little did I know, she was to cut all of her cords here and completely disappear out of my life.

I have never heard from her again. In the beginning, I was at a loss; she was the one person I could count on to talk about the spirit world here. I was psychically on my own. This ended up strengthening my relationship with my son and turn towards my inner self when I saw and heard things inexplicable.

Several days later, I was taking a bath in my second floor bathroom underneath the attic and something drew me to look out the window and I saw this huge, black demon spirit in broad daylight moving around the house, over the roof, and then back down to the ground, trying to find a way in.

The crystal shield of protection from Jesus Christ and the protection from Archangel Michael will always be here. I thought this was like a live *Harry Potter* movie. I laughed and felt no fear.

I later on cried as this demon spirit lured my cat, Eva—that I had rescued at three months' old in an old, abandoned house—was lured out on the roof by my office upstairs next to the attic. I caught her just in time, she had suffered a complete nervous breakdown from the evilness of this demon and was almost comatose.

Eva hid in the east wing alcove for a week; wouldn't eat or drink or come downstairs. She had been absolutely terrified.

I took her to a veterinarian who confirmed the cat had had a terrifying experience and a nervous breakdown from something very scary, and she gave me a mother cat pheromone dispenser and told me to keep her in my bedroom with the door closed and see if she would recover. It took Eva several months to leave my room she has finally fully recovered.

Around July 2018, I had a sixth sense a spirit was following me around the house and the grounds for several days and was giving me the creeps like he was stalking me. I strangely felt he just loved to look at my naked body.

I had been flea bombing room by room and enjoyed walking around the grounds and watching the birds. I had just one flea bomb left in the kitchen pantry locked in a cabinet. I had a nice morning except that creepy feeling someone was watching me.

I went to pick up Ryan from his volunteer job at the Bread for Life Food Bank at Saint Therese Catholic Church. When we got back home, I went to use the bathroom in my bedroom and my bedroom door was closed, I knew I left it open so the cats could use the litter box in the butler's pantry off the kitchen. A flea bomb had just been set off with my cat hiding under the bed. Those evil spirits are so sneaky, no one else was on the farm.

I asked Ryan if he saw a spirit or ghost in the house and he replied it was Blackbeard; the pirate had entered the house when he went to work that morning and had been watching me all day.

I asked Ryan where he was now and he said he went into the stable. I took Ryan in the car and drove to the barn and asked Ryan where he was.

Ryan said that he was sitting in front of my desk in my stable office, in my chair. I walked into my office and snapped a photo. I told Ryan we were going to call upon Jesus Christ and Archangel Michael to release his spirit and ban him from the farm and so we did.

His picture showed up in my photograph. I'm not surprised Blackbeard pirates traded with the Powhatan Indians, the French, and the Brits in this cove. Ryan said for days, Blackbeard was the evilest ghost he had come across and still get shivers if you even say his name.

I took Ryan back home and Brenda the tenant in the one-bedroom guest cottage next to my kitchen which I named the hobbit house came over complaining she had rats in her attic at night and the noise kept waking up.

I said to myself it's probably a ghost and asked her if I could come and see. I went into her house and took the fold down ladder from the attic and went upstairs, I didn't smell or see any rats or mice but saw the ghost of an elderly man named Bill who was Charlie Carruthers caretaker and lived and died in the hobbit house.

Bill wanted the house all to himself and was wreaking havoc in Brenda's house to make her leave. I smiled at Bill, went back downstairs, and told Brenda it must have been a squirrel that got trapped in the attic and went home.

I told Ryan I needed him to go tell Bill the ghost to stop bothering Brenda and so he did.

I felt I needed to take Ryan to another psychic so I could have her ask him some questions in the way psychics communicate, as I felt Ryan needed to learn to cleanse and ground his energy field and be able to shield himself from other energies and share more things with me.

I found an angelic psychic medium near Portsmouth and made an appointment for Ryan. I went with him to her office and she instantly was pleased she told me Ryan was very close with God.

She said Ryan had three angels from God with him at all times; their names were Teresa, James, and Linda. We chatted about some of the experiences that we had had at Eagle Point Plantation, and I told her I thought Ryan was meant to be a spirit releaser and I felt that Archangel Michael and Archangel Metatron were training him, which she confirmed.

She told me that the only thing that ever-scared Ryan was his encounter with Blackbeard, the pirate. I never told her about Blackbeard before this. She said I was very well protected by God and Jesus Christ and another angel that Jesus Christ had sent to watch over me, who shows up in my photos but is not supposed to communicate with me; although, he lends me his strength constantly around the farm.

She announced Ryan and I would have no fear and that Ryan would probably be at home until he was 22 years old and at that time, he would develop more mental telepathy with me.

She told me that my past lives and spiritual ascension would kick in in June of my 52nd year, and that it would all make sense to me at that time.

She also told me that Ryan spends all of his time out of his body in God's garden or Behind the Veil, which I now understand and have more compassion for Ryan's rituals of bathing and napping and waking up with ethereal joy and peace on his face. She had answered and confirmed my intuition and my answers and questions and Ryan had enjoyed his time with her and her angelic aura.

This meeting helped me and Ryan bond more and he was more open to me and would announce the times that he was going to talk to God with a huge smile.

Ryan tells me that his conversations with God were a secret and we would make games out of it, laughing. Did you see Jesus Christ here last night and Archangel Michael and Archangel Raphael and we also have archangel Uriel in Archangel Gabriel.

In the next few days, the marine police showed up in front of my house and said that they had a mayday signal coming from inside my house.

I let them search the house and the grounds on foot and by boat. They could not find a boat or a radio anywhere.

They searched my tenant's homes for radios and they searched the neighbor's homes for radios and found nothing.

They left stumped and upset. At the end of the night before we were going to sleep, the marine police showed up again with the police and the fire department, they told me they received another mayday signal from inside the plantation.

The marine police officer told me he was very concerned about me and Ryan's safety and they combed the grounds on foot and with boats and couldn't find anyone or a radio.

The Marine police officer left afraid for me, I put the horses to bed and then we had a terrible thunderstorm with another power outage. It is not a fun feeling to have a police officer tell you they fear for your safety.

Agitated, I asked my next-door neighbor to come and search all the catacombs in the basement and the closets and secret trap ways in the middle and east wings with a flashlight.

We found nothing. I did not sleep well that night. I never heard from the marine police again and for weeks after this experience, I kept hearing a voice saying, *mayday, mayday,* that would send shivers down my spine. It must have been a pirate ghost or a demon, eventually it went away. Satan and his demons will not stop at any cost.

Hurricane season 2018.
Being from California, we have earthquakes and wildfires. The East Coast has hurricanes. I had been watching the hurricane forecast and we were in for a direct hit with a category 4 hurricane.

I was nervous; I had eight horses boarded was not prepared to move them and didn't have the money to go and evacuate anywhere.

The night before the storm was supposed to hit, a tenant that lives next door to me came over and knocked on my kitchen door and told me that we had a mandatory evacuation immediately.

My heart sank; I told him I was staying I couldn't leave my horses. All of the tenants on the property evacuated. Ryan and I were alone. I was sitting on my back porch watching the sunset and I saw a vision of God and his face; our Heavenly Father shown down on me.

It was a sign of assurance that Ryan and I were safe and God and His angels have control over the weather. I instantly felt relaxed and safe and loved.

The storm decreased to a tropical depression by the time it arrived at Eagle Point, we had 50 mile an hour winds, lost power for 3 days and lost several hundred-year-old trees and 200-feet of pasture board fencing in my horses pasture.

The next morning, I asked Ryan if he wanted to go to McDonald's for breakfast and of course, he said yes. I asked him if he saw God last night and he replied, "Yes, I did," smiling.

I had been obsessed taking videos of the different colored stars and rays around them above the cove, the photos Maryanne had said were extraterrestrial markers.

I had always suspected that they have their own colony in the sky and underground. Ryan always asked me not to photograph them as they tried to communicate with him and their vibration was a crushing horrible feeling.

On August 17th, 2018, I was on my back porch and Archangel Metatron appeared and spoke to my guardian angel and said that an extraterrestrial spacecraft needed to make an emergency landing right next to my master bedroom and to tell Kristin. I said, "Okay, as long as they cloak themselves, I don't want NASA here, or an alien war here."

I have many videos of this illuminating, green spacecraft and I'm always in wonder. My sixth sense was telling me that Satan was trying to make allies with other galaxies to form an army to destroy Earth and humanity.

These other civilizations above my cove are cloaked and guarded by God's angels and watched over by Archangel Metatron and Archangel Michael.

One day, I was driving on the other end of town and I had a hunch that I wanted to take some photographs of the backside of Eagle Point from Bray's Landing Road in Guinea. We drove there and I took some photographs of Eagle Point, the house and the coves.

When I got back home, I put on my eyeglasses to look at the pictures. One of them showed two tank-looking vehicles with cords that disappeared into the sky. Of course, they were extraterrestrial ground vehicles next to my swimming pool.

Of course, I can't see them myself when I walk out by the pool but they are undeniably in the photographs, and I thought to myself, *Oh well, we have God, Jesus Christ and the archangels here.*

The angels have portals all over my house and grounds. We are blessed with violet sunrises and when the sun shines on the cove, it dazzles like millions of diamonds, like God is pouring divine crystalline holy diamonds filling up the river. I always think God is blessing us, shining heaven on Earth on this special place.

Out of the blue, there will be thousands of ospreys and seagulls and flocks of blackbirds swirling around the house and then disappearing into thin air and sometimes when you look up to heaven the clouds will part and holy rays of golden light will flood the house and grounds and then turn rainbow colors and then disappear.

I tried to stay away from videoing the extraterrestrials except for every once in a while. Some of the spirits out there don't show up in the photographs, and I will find out on Easter of 2019 why.

You can see Jesus Christ's crystal shield around the house it shines like magic. Even my horses, Zeus, Coconut and Zachary, have their own beautiful, white winged angel guarding them in their stable.

Ryan and I have so much fun sharing these things together. The archangels communicate with light and sound and birds.

I have hundreds of pictures of the beautiful angels here; they will tap on a window if I'm supposed to see something.

Archangel Michael came to me on my back porch one night and shared with me that this plantation home and the grounds have been raked over the coals for thousands of years and is full of death and spirits not to mention layers and layers of vibration underneath the land from the Pirates and the Indians. Then he chuckled and said why did you have to choose a civil war slave plantation and disappeared.

Every day here is an experience filled with magic. I have never felt so much love, peace, joy, and harmony inside these walls; which is Jesus Christ's presence, he is the king here.

I keep a daily journal of my experiences here and of my dreams. I have had so many prolific dreams from the angels about my past and present and other people in my life, it is like putting a thousand-piece jigsaw puzzle together.

I needed this healing to rid myself of negative attachments from past lives and to balance my emotions to become whole with Jesus Christ to write this book. It has been a year of the angels working with me and God fully encourages me to write this book about his son Jesus Christ and his angels.

I use the book *Animal Spirit Guides* by Stephen D. Farmer, PhD, as a guide to the animals the angels use to show me signs and guide myself.

In the middle of winter, hundreds of dragonflies would show up in front of my kitchen door and then disappear. Dragonfly is a sign that the mystery of life is reawakening for you, recharge your psychic energy as you are going through a major transformation in life.

They tamed and sent four wild mallard ducks that live in my barn now with my horses as a reminder to laugh every day, and feel joy, peace and harmony in the stress of everyday life. Duck is the symbol of fertility, either literally or metaphorically.

On September 26th we had a beautiful full moon and I saw a vision of Jesus Christ above the dock pool area as a reassurance that he and the angels are healing and protecting Ryan and I from the extra-terrestrial sphere. Incredible, divine love and overwhelming peaceful I thought to myself, the Lord has shown me so much compassion and mercy, and most of the time Ryan and I are here alone helpless which is why God has blessed us with so many angels.

One of my favorite books is *Jesus the Christ* by James Tallmadge. After reading this book, I was overwhelmed with such intense emotion and sadness of humanities faith and what a huge heart and overwhelming love and kindness Jesus Christ had for the people on this Earth.

It seems the mentality of most of the human race is still based on demanding instant miracles of abundance. Jesus Christ created the word *abundance* as 'time to be at peace with nature and God's creatures and to be able to perform acts of kindness', not instant wealth and success.

The next morning, we were blessed with a magnificent violet sunrise shining fuchsia and gold light illuminating the cove from heaven and flocks of thousands of seagulls, and hundreds of Canadian geese in front of the house a sign of love from God.

In November, severe thunderstorms brought us a power outage. This house is so quiet without electricity and also very dark. When the wind blows through the singing stairs upstairs next to my office, the stairs sing and whistle.

Another vision of Jesus Christ outside my kitchen that night he shown his violet flame through my soul. Surreal, peaceful and yes Ryan and I live in another realm in itself.

11/11. Prolific dreams this morning, something to do with my past lives in the Great Lakes of Ohio and Oregon. My daughter Ashley came and visited and we had a beautiful Sunday. Ryan shared with me that the 11:11 sign is a test from God if you are aware of his angels' presence.

Particularly very high vibrational frequency here today filled with joy and peace and angel guidance of omnipresence is the key to divine love from Archangel Michael, beautiful.

This evening, Ryan was irritated that the extraterrestrials were attempting to communicate with him through telepathy.

Angels everywhere tonight in this home and grounds, Ryan announced that he was going to talk to God this evening. I went to bed early in peace. Ryan's conversations with God and Jesus Christ are private and I respect that.

The next morning Ryan and I were blessed with another beautiful, gold sunrise with Archangel Metatron and Archangel Raphael by our front door dormer with the yard full of snow geese, blue and white herons and white cranes; a sign from God and Jesus Christ shining love and light down on me and Ryan.

Important message of faith. Today, Ryan shared with me on the way to the school bus, that he is an angel and I believe him.

Through the holidays would be a huge emotional healing experience for me and strengthening the bond that Ryan and I have which is irreplaceable and magical in itself.

A few days later, I received Ryan's test results from his appointment at the VCU cancer survivor program in the mail. The test results said he had a tumor in his heart and signs of lung cancer. I was sitting in my car sobbing beside myself.

I went into the kitchen as so not to upset Ryan and I could hear the angels asking why I was crying and then they knew. I felt their pink love surrounding me with strength and compassion and pure love for Ryan. I somehow managed to pull myself together and call his doctor for some answers; she was out of town and I begged for another doctor to call me immediately my nerves and concern for Ryan couldn't wait.

About an hour later, I received a call from another oncologist that told me that the typist had failed to put the word negative in the results. I thanked him and sat in awe and wonder over the miracle Jesus Christ had performed, saving Ryan from cancer. I sat for several days in pure joy and overwhelming love for God, Jesus Christ, and his angels.

The next night, Ryan bathed for an unusually long time, I sensed the angels were cleansing his body and he was visiting Jesus Christ. Still emotionally drained, I was given signs to feed Ryan more organic food and encourage him to exercise to keep his physical body in health.

The next morning, we had a heavenly, violet sunrise filled with peace, joy, and harmony. Ryan's vibration and the angelic frequency was very high today and he's been very open communicating with me.

In quiet meditation, Jesus Christ sent me a message through my guardian angel that I was guided to Eagle Point by God, and it was in my path in life to cleanse this home and these grounds from the demons—and it was Satan that had orchestrated the conjuring of last year—and to rise above fear and strengthen my faith and my relationship with Jesus Christ.

Contemplation of thoughts on negative emotions, jealousy, envy, greed, unhealthy relationships and how to achieve purity in living in divine light and love.

More prolific dreams and emotional healing. I'm particularly sensitive to Stewart's negative energy and energy from others, preferring to be in solitude on the farm with my horses, birds and Ryan.

This year, Ryan and I are focusing on a *grande* Christmas to honor Jesus Christ and his angels. We had a beautiful, peaceful Thanksgiving this year. I love Thanksgiving and love to decorate early for the holidays.

It is amazing when you have faith that prayers are answered by God.

My Belgian draft horse Zeus had come down with a deadly case laminitis. I locked him in his stall for 6 days, treating him with bute and isoxsuprine. I prayed several times daily to Jesus Christ. I had raised Zeus from five months old and he is now 13 years old.

I am somewhat of a horse whisperer; my horses follow me closely without halters and we share a deep unconditional love.
Ryan and I spent a lot of time talking during the Thanksgiving weekend. I asked Ryan if he had one wish in the world would it be to cure his autism and he replied, "No, I love who I am and I am a lightworker on a holy level with a divinely high vibration and communicate with angelic realm." He said, "I don't experience the negative emotions of the ego." Ryan doesn't experience jealousy, envy, greed or hate or dishonesty; he is holy. And the only confidence issues he has are negative feedback from insensitive teachers. I like to video us together saying our prayers in front of our bride mirror, watching his angels.

The next morning, Ryan went back to school and we were blessed with another magical sunrise. Driving to the school bus, radiating gold and diamond rays beaming down around us in the front yard filled with dozens of white storks. This is pure love from God and Jesus Christ.

After the bus picked up Ryan, I went to the stable to give Zeus his medication. Zeus had that gleam in his eye he was touched by the Lord. I decided to put his halter on and see if he can make it out of his stall. He whinnied and kissed my cheek and walked out of his stall in the barn aisle 100% sound.

I put him out in his pasture and noticed there were thousands and thousands of ospreys swirling above his pasture and barn. I lifted my arms up to the sky and danced in circles watching the birds and then the birds disappeared into thin air. I instantly prayed in gratitude to Jesus Christ; he had granted me another miracle and cured Zeus from a deadly case and laminitis.

Waves of joy, peace and harmony overcame me. I would find later on that there were a group of three spirit ladies that resided in the sunset rental house next to my stable hundreds of years ago that practiced witchcraft and performed hexes.

I decided on a 15-foot cedar tree from our yard to cut for the dining room for Christmas. I went to town decorating the house and tree.

Ryan and I went to habitat for humanity and bought dozens of beautiful angel figurines with hand-sewn velvet gowns and sequins.

It took me three weeks to finish the tree and decorate the farm. My daughter Ashley is a Christmas day baby so I always make a big event out of this holiday.

One night, I was saying my prayers in my 2nd floor bathroom under the attic and had left my voice recorder on. I was thinking how close and blessed Ryan is by our Heavenly Father. The next morning, I listened to the video, it was in the beautiful Angelic realm with the angels singing. Breathtaking, we were going to have a blessed holiday this year.

More prolific dreams from my childhood, releasing guilt and regret over bad decisions I had made in the past; being a single parent since my children were three and four years old. My children haven't spoken to their father since they were five and six nor did he ever pay any child support know nor do we know where his.

More prolific dreams that next morning of the obstacles I had incurred in my life and of Stewart wanting me to participate in group sex with other women in my dream. I removed my soul for my body and just spectated.

I was happy to see Stewart go off to his home in Gladys. I enjoyed the peace cleaning my stalls that morning and walked back to the house to take a bath and Jesus Christ had left a very large, white angel feather at the foot of the staircase; beautiful.

Several days later, preparing for Christmas, I drove Ryan to the school bus and we were shown the most beautiful, male, white-winged angel flying to the stable. Ryan was very pleased with this as he knows how much I love my horses.

I am so glad the full moon energy is waning. This morning, the angels guided me on a dream to find a magic potion; rough path but no fear or anger. Christmas Eve, my morning dreams, I was in a foreign country gathering coins with my ancestors.

Beautiful day full of peace. Ryan and I spent the whole day cleaning and dusting the house and last-minute present wrapping to prepare for Christmas.

Christmas morning, we were blessed with the most magical gold and violet sunrise filled with peace, joy, and harmony. Ryan loved his Christmas presents and we had a beautiful Christmas dinner with candlelight and Ryan's angels and I said a special grace blessing with gratitude and love to Jesus Christ and a special handmade cross cake that I had made. Stewart and Ashley talked for a long time while I did the dishes and everyone had a great time.

Stewart and I had hot steamy sex in the morning and took a nap afterwards. I made everyone brunch and Stewart headed back home to Gladys and Ryan and I rested and enjoyed each other's conversations. Ryan shared with me that Jesus Christ had visited him on Christmas night and that it was our secret.

One of my psychic friends drew a woodpecker tarot card for me which says, *My heart beats with Mother Earth and this is so true.*

My guardian angel and Jesus Christ had guided me to Eagle Point. This farm is a holy place filled with peace and harmony, emanating everywhere from heaven to Mother Earth.

Several days later I was standing on my front porch off the kitchen cooking dinner after a long stressful day with Stewart demands and unkind unloving narcissistic behavior towards me and Ryan and I glanced up at the sky and a heavenly beam of golden and diamond white light shine right down from heaven through my soul unconditional pure divine love from Jesus Christ.

The plantation house is very sensitive to the people that live here energies and the energy of the antiques and other things that are decorated here.
I had found two handmade hummingbird pictures from Aztec made with real hummingbird feathers; an art called plumeria that were made in the 1700s that I had on a bookcase in my bedroom. I woke up in the middle of the night and the bookcase shelf that the bird pictures were on started rattling and the bird pictures literally flew off the shelf onto the floor and then the bookcase shelf flew off onto the floor.

I didn't think too much of it; I'm very well protected and put the bookcase shelf back and replaced the bird pictures.

Two minutes after I went back to bed, the same thing happened. For some reason, I turned on the night-light and put my reading glasses on and read the back of the bird picture frames that I never noticed before. The pictures were made for an Aztec god. That's the answer; they were made by an Aztec witch practitioner and her energy was still on those pictures, confirmed by a psychic friend of mine.

It was Archangel Michael protecting me and removing negative energy from the house, ebb and flow, emotional twist my heart will grow with more love with more spiritual growth and to not ever have an object in the house that represents another god or idol but the Lord Jesus Christ.

The next morning Ryan and I were treated once again to one of God's magical sunrises filled with love, peace, joy and harmony. We had a quiet and peaceful New Year's Eve.

Quiet contemplation over my relationship with Jesus Christ. He saved my son from cancer and saved me from self-sabotage and that Jesus Christ and Archangel Michael had saved me and Ryan from the demons in this home. God, Jesus Christ the archangels and all of his angels are so magical filled with divine love and light and Ryan and I are truly blessed by them.

The next morning, Ryan and I were blessed again with another magical golden sunrise from God. Today is epiphany. I spent the whole day chalking the doors with Holy Spirit and chalices and doves. I baked a cross cake in honor of Jesus Christ and cooked a feast for Ryan and myself. We had a beautiful dinner with candles incense and Ryan's angels. After dinner, Ryan and I heard Jesus Christ's angels singing and playing the trumpet outside the dining room announcing his arrival that night for a special visit with Ryan.

I went and rode my horses and came back home and was escorted to my second-floor bathroom by one of his angels, took a bath and went right to sleep as requested.

The next morning, there was a beautiful, large, white angel feather; a gift from Jesus Christ on my bedroom floor. I had beautiful dreams from my spirit guides last night telling me that I am a beautiful soul. Have fun, relax and enjoy the peace and harmony here and make friends.

I asked Ryan later about his visit with Jesus Christ and as usual, he said it was a secret. So very magical time on the farm for the next few days with more prolific dreams cutting ethereal chords, emotional healing and messages from the angels about the tenants' personality; as close to heaven on Earth as possible.

The lunar energy really affects us here at Eagle Point. I had a peaceful walk to the stable this morning and was treated with literally thousands and thousands of osprey birds swirling above the stable and pastures and the beautiful white-winged male angel that protects my horses showed himself to me in the tractor barn.

I just stood under the birds, swirling everywhere like I was going in and out of a vortex. I laughed with pure joy twirling around myself as I watched them; they disappeared into thin air.

Jesus Christ and his angels have brought heaven to Earth here at this beautiful, old plantation. The Archangels continue to cleanse the 400-acre grounds of any negative chords and demon spirits. A beautiful day full of peace and harmony. Archangel Metatron continues to work with Ryan developing his psychic skills.

Ryan prefers the company of his angels and God himself. I dreamt last night that my mother's feelings were hurt; she wasn't feeling loved by her family. I sent her flowers this morning and she really appreciated it. My cats were tense to noises in the house this cold winter, most likely post-traumatic stress disorder from last year's events. We are looking forward to Spring.

Life is about energy and faith transmitted from Archangel Michael through a reverend angel communicator. Love, light and intention; open heart to feel emotions; transformation of the Earth; sacred contract and free will of actions and to use psychic gifts; increase faith and intuition and to co-create spiritual powers; love and light. Birds everywhere.

A few days later, Stewart showed up as a demon himself. My guides told me this was not going to be an enjoyable visit from him and Ryan's angels didn't want Stewart near him. Thankfully, the angels made him sleep all day and after a very tough night's sleep, with the angels showing me that Stewart is capable of murder, I remembered that Jesus Christ had told me in the stable that he could not break Stewart's contract, who must be with Satan.

Thankfully, under God's will he left that day. Ryan spent the day with God, cosmic aligning. I was told to nurture myself by my guardian angel. We had thousands of seagulls, ospreys and Canadian geese in the yard; beautiful. I love and forgive myself; I love Jesus Christ and his angels.

As time goes on Stewart will spend less and less time here as "he hath spoken." It is God's will and during this time I will regain my inner strength, intuition, self-love and spirituality.

My guardian angel tells me that I am brave and have warrior strength. I have come used to their very high vibration and very much enjoyed being with Ryan although he will be called at 4 am at times to bathe and prepare himself for the archangel's visit, which always wakes me up too. I will adjust and be more sensitive to this in the future. I woke up with a strange body vibration this morning and my heart racing. I went into the kitchen and saw a beautiful, pink angel, Jesus Christ's angel, and I took a photo and also showed Archangel Metatron next to Jesus's angel.

I looked out the kitchen window and saw thousands of seagulls and ospreys bathed in golden rays. This made me laugh and smile; the angels are so much fun and this cured my ailments instantly. Ryan would be visited again by Jesus Christ tonight.

That evening, the angels took me to heaven's garden in my dreams. So breathtakingly magical, beautiful, holy, peace, pristine fields of flowers everywhere mixed with bountiful vegetables and fruits and baby birds and animals all over the place. I was in absolute awe. As I awoke, I thanked the Lord.

That night, I dreamt about female spirit goddesses making love and gorillas running all around the house. A sign to have more self-respect and a heightened sense of clairaudience and love of Mother Earth. I would have more prolific dreams over the next few days as it is Jesus Christ's will for my guides and angels to cut more ethereal negative cords from my past lives and to heal my soul with divine love and light.

The next day, I had a very vivid dream that I was walking down a road on my path from a past life and there was a male, Spanish conquistador on a white Lipizzaner horse that kept cornering me and blocking me with his dancing horse from my path.

I felt no fear and managed to escape him. I woke up in peace. The angels gave me a reprieve of peace with Stewart over the next few days he was actually kind, loving, compassionate. We had great sex and rekindled our romance, I really enjoyed his company.

We enjoyed four days and three nights together, he took us shopping and then he said he was sad to leave and how much he loved me.

I had a peaceful day and took Coconut on a moonlight trail ride and I could hear the vibration of a new spacecraft near the cove. That night, I dreamt the house was full of grizzly bears and gorillas and a giant serpent. Archangel Michael loves to play with grizzly bears. I woke up in the middle of the night and a voice guided me to the east wing of the house which had been sealed off since winter. I went up with no light and the same spirits of the Bryant family and the O'Grady family were still there as they always will be.

I took a few more pictures and came back downstairs to my bedroom and went on my back porch to get some fresh air and Archangel Michael appeared next to me laughing with me and told me I was brave and fearless and I had finally connected with faith.

I slept blissfully through the rest of the night. The next morning, I woke up to peace, joy, and harmony. I had a relaxing day and I thought of and how much I love my life and God's holy land here with his archangels and Jesus Christ.

That afternoon, we were blessed with Archangel Uriel around the grounds healing hundreds of years of chaos, death, murder and deceit in the land. He brings thousands and thousands of flocks of blackbirds, absolutely beautiful.

The next day, I dreamt when I was a little girl, my father took me to a horse show and I always had a little baby boy with me that was not Ryan. This child had an ethereal cord attached to me that Archangel Michael removed. Signs of a new beginning of my spirit connecting with spirituality, sexuality, and vulnerability. I woke up feeling enlightened and was treated to falcons all over the backyard with Archangel Uriel.

That night I had a beautiful moonlight trail ride on Coconut and Zeus had injured his eye and was very upset and in pain. I cried and gave him some medicine and slathered his eye with ointment and kissed him and gave him carrots and apples.

I went home to bed prayed to Jesus Christ to protect him and wrap angel wings around him in his sleep. I was woken up in the middle of the night into the angelic realm with the angels singing, Ryan would be visiting with God this night.

The next morning Ryan and I were blessed with another magical morning heaven on earth and literally thousands and thousands of Ospreys and seagulls all over the farm.

Ryan and I smiled and giggled at each other as I took him to the school bus, I truly love and respect Ryan with all of my heart. I went to the stable and the angels had healed Zeus's eye. I thanked God, Jesus Christ the archangels and angels with grace, gratitude, and love and spent the entire day outside enjoying the peacocks, squirrels, raccoons and the view of the river.

Ryan and I are truly blessed; it is a truly amazing the feeling of unconditional love the mother experiences with her children and animals and with God and Jesus Christ.

The next day, I was compelled to research Jonathan Bryant who had renamed the little pine island next to the cove: The Jonathan Bryant family graveyard. He was very high up ranking in the confederate army and was very close with Robert E. Lee.

I became fascinated reading about him not only was he on the King's Council in Richmond, he had a very close personal relationship with God and was actually in the scriptures. Ryan and I had a peaceful day and I rode Coconut and Zeus under the moonlight that night.

The angels showed me I had lived here at Eagle Point Plantation in a past lifetime. I had a huge pain of heart-wrenching emotion over Jesus Christ and how cruel humanity is. I literally saw him and cried all night; my true love and faith to him. It is almost as if I was with him through his crucifixion and pain and suffering from the cruelty of humanity and I was.

The next morning, Ryan and I were blessed with another one of God's magical violet sunrises and also the sound of what was like an army of UFOs over the pool and cove. I did not share that part with Ryan when I took him to school.

And I felt at divine peace, grateful of experiencing such emotion over Jesus Christ who will always be the king of Eagle Point and the Earth, and of our hearts and souls. Thank you to the angels.

The next day, I had another very prolific dream. Thank you, Archangel Michael and Archangel Raphael, for cutting cords from the witch's spirit in the sunset house, the rental next to me. I called her Kathy.

She had tried to put a spell of addiction on me. I woke up at 3 am, 4 am, and 5:30 am, and then the angels took me into the sunset house and showed me their magic, almost like spraying the entire inside of the house with divine whipped cream that turned into white doves and flew out. Beautiful, what a treat, thank you so very much archangels.

The next day, planting a fruit orchard to sow seeds to Earth, God shined golden divine rays of love with thousands of birds swirling within His rays; divine, peace, joy, and harmony.

The angels guided me to have a psychic friend of mine read my mother's picture as she has suddenly taken deathly ill and was suffering from severe panic attacks.

My friend told me my mother had died at Eagle Point in a past life as well and had an evil demon on her and a hex from a witch. I paid for my mother to go to an angelic spirit releaser at the Green Man near her in Burbank.

Beautiful, violet, sunrise with pink clouds; deep gratitude to Jesus Christ for his guidance.

I slept very hard that night and the angels sent a peacock to my bedroom door to wake me up. Ryan would be in God's garden all day.

Magical sunset surrounded with violet rays, gold rays and rainbow rays emanating from the Sun surrounding me. I felt very connected spiritually tonight and on this full snow moon.

Archangel Michael cut another negative female ethereal cord from me. I love you, archangel Michael. The next morning's sunrise had a golden cross extending from heaven to below Earth illuminating divine golden Ray's over the cove, I was in absolute awe. Ryan and I smiled at each other.

Peaceful day, I smiled when the angels sent cranky Stewart home. Rode both of my horses in peace tonight and Archangel Michael removed more negative attachments from my past.

We were expecting a big snowstorm the next day. I love snow but I can't drive my car and dread walking back and forth to the stable or if we have a power outage. Ironically, it snowed everywhere in Gloucester and Hayes, over a foot of snow, and the sun shone down on Eagle Point; not even a drop of rain. Thank you, God.

The next morning, I had a bizarre dream of a very large black man riding an owl the size of a dinosaur. Ryan and Archangel Michael were in the east wing cleansing energy off the old antique furniture Stewart recently brought here.

I have been resolving guilt issues about moving to Virginia and leaving my family; guilt over how my horses are in heaven here with their grass pastures and double size stalls, releasing resentment over my ex-husbands non-existent part of my children's life, both emotionally and financially.

Ryan never speaks of his dad, God and Jesus Christ are his father and his family. It is amazing how much more self-love you have when you forgive yourself for your decisions in life and ignore the ego mind and allow yourself to heal by releasing negative emotions and let pure, unconditional, love into your heart and soul; this is discovering your higher self, and a sign of pure faith to God and Jesus Christ, the archangels and the angels. Very much gratitude, Archangel Michael, how hard you work with me; I love you.

I let my mind wander, creating beautiful, decorating themes for this house. I fantasize about painting the dining room cherry red with an al fresco of Jesus Christ and his angels on the ceiling, and a floor-to-ceiling mural of Jesus

Christ and his angels on the soaring second floor hallway, and stained-glass windows of Archangel Michael and Archangel Metatron above the singing stairs.

I would decorate the rest of the house in French provincial with pale-pink creams and gold, gold columns in the vestibule in the front entrance and flowers everywhere.

I would put a huge fountain in the circular driveway with angel statues and a Mother Mary statue with a boxwood and rose garden and yes, also a cross.

I had a pleasant night horseback riding and increasingly intense emotions over Jesus Christ. That night in my dreams, I continued to confess my sins and the angels showed me one of my tenants was a drug dealer, which I suspected he doesn't live here, and uses the house as some type of laboratory; then comes here maybe one hour a week.

I had a horrible afternoon and night with Ryan the next day, he gets very upset with me organizing his room and teaching him how to clean. Yes, he will improve later on and thank you to his angels Teresa, Linda, and James for helping me with this.

Eventually, he would give in and ask me to go clean his room every day while he was in school.

We cleaned until 9 pm that night and I decided to go out and ride my horses in the freezing weather. Then my mother texted me she was going to commit suicide and Stewart sent me a hateful text saying he didn't love me anymore. I had way too much stress today.

The next morning, I just cried. I cried and sobbed all day; I give so much love and nurturing to Stewart and Ryan; they don't realize how hard I try and that I get tired and need some nurturing back. Ryan is an empath, also going through puberty. Stewart is a classic psychic vampire.

I needed to make some changes in my life. First off, every time Stewart walks in the door, to ask Archangel Michael to put a shield 10-foot wide around me and Ryan and secondly to have more time for me and Ryan to have fun and let loose.

I'm very proud of Ashley making a career change to work at a private, nonprofit special needs children's school. She is a natural healer and an empath and highly intelligent. She graduated high school at 16 and earned enough college credits for a bachelor's degree by 19.

I spent the day relaxing with my horses and my cats; they are my therapy. That night, I was exhausted. My eyes were swollen and my muscles were tired. I went upstairs to my nightly bath and the angels had left a beautiful, golden feather at the bottom of the stairs. This really cheered me up as the angels always do. I love my guardian angel; he gives me his strength and guides and protect me always. Appreciation, love, and gratitude, beautiful angels.

It's amazing how Jesus Christ can affect your life when you give up your free will and ask him for his guidance.

Stewart started to have some compassion for me and Ryan is enjoying being spoiled by his mom and loving his special training with Archangel Michael and Archangel Metatron and his visits with God. My mother is causing me stress; she refuses to go to the angelic spirit releaser I asked her to go to.

This would cause her long and drawn-out suffering, battling breast and stomach cancer.

Ryan and I had a peaceful night and the next morning, Ryan and I were treated to thousands and thousands of angels everywhere in the house and grounds. Surreal, beautiful, blessed, peace, joy and harmony, heaven on Earth.

The sunset that night was so beautiful, gold and diamond rays of light shining on the kitchen with hundreds of seagulls swirling within bathed in light; a sign that Jesus Christ was with us today filling us with divine love.

And again, the next night, a brilliant sunset; gold and diamond rays shining through my body as I sat on the kitchen porch that turn to green, jade, pink and blue rays shining through my crown chakra. Healing pink, violet, and gold and white, and then green. Thousands of blackbirds everywhere; Archangel Uriel, thank you.

The next day, we were blessed with a pure angelic realm vibration. I went upstairs to my office and a ladybug and landed on my hand in 30 degree weather; a sign that Mother Mary would protect me as I was in for an awful night with Stewart who screamed at me for over an hour for no reason projecting his anger, jealousy and self-loathing at me and Ryan for no reason other than he lives in fear and greed.

Most of Stewart's resentment towards me is due to problems with his business and he can't control me like he did before and he is not happy with my relationship with Jesus Christ.

Thankfully, he left. I had a beautiful ride on my Belgians and Ryan and I laughed; even Elizabeth O'Grady spirit in my library doesn't like Stewart either. God, Jesus Christ and his angels protected me in my sleep, I could feel their wings around me and they told me I will be very successful and happy and find friends and true love in the future.

Beautiful, peaceful sleep, even Ryan's angels are shining pink love on me and Mother Mary's violet flame shining down on me.

Ryan and I were blessed to a beautiful violet and fuchsia sunrise and my spirit guides showed me for mallard duck—take care of my own emotional needs, dream lighten up and laugh, this will manifest my goal. Love and light manifests all.

That night, I astral traveled with Ashley and Ryan on a roller-coaster water slide, we had so much fun and then Ashley and Ryan were riding bulls with western saddles on them. Spirit sign-fertility, creativity, upturn, prosperity and set goals and commit. This was the sign from the angels.

I had a rough afternoon with Ryan that day; he wanted to talk to God instantly. I had some mercy from Jesus Christ, he left another beautiful, white feather on my bed.

The next morning, we had a beautiful sunrise, there were literally thousands of seagulls swirling above the house; a sign from God. Beautiful morning filled with joy, peace, and harmony and more angels here than ever; we are truly blessed by the Holy Spirit and Jesus Christ here.

Today, the hawks were kiting around the house for hours, an important message from spirit to protect myself from psychic attacks and ground my energy.

It's been like paradise here all day and that night, a beautiful white-winged male angel escorted me upstairs to my bathroom while Ryan was visiting with Jesus Christ in his room. Overwhelming joy.

The next morning, I had a prolific dream about Zeus following me up a golden spiral staircase up to heaven. We went up at twice, while all the others were going down, I felt no fear. This was a sign to follow my intuition, be creative and enjoy life.

I had a beautiful ride on my horses that night singing *Hallelujah*. The next morning, I had another prolific dream from one of my ancestors that is a sorcerer that had battled Satan and he wanted to show me that he will always be there with me.

Was this a premonition of the future? The angels are telling me that some area of this house has not been cleared of negative energy and the library comes to my mind; it would be hidden behind the walls of the library cabinets that the Carruthers installed in 2003. This will come into play in the future.

The next morning, I had a dream that I was supposed to write a screenplay about my experience at Eagle Point and it would be a bigger hit than a Harry Potter movie as it is real.

Eagle Point Plantation is God's land and Jesus Christ is the king here. I had a day full of harmony and faith, I mowed the lawn all night with no demands on my time and then went on a trail ride.

Ryan shared with me today that he was taken to heaven while he was in the hospital with cancer and he began his love with God in Jesus Christ and that he was baptized by the Holy Ghost and taken through all the realms of heavens and shown everything just like Enoch, the Archangel Metatron.

He then shared with me that it was the 30 days of radiation aimed towards his pineal gland that opened his third eye and his speech and he was very happy here. I am so happy Ryan is opening up to me, we love each other very much. That night, Jesus Christ sent an angel cocooning me in my sleep very, very close. This is God's land and I'm writing his book.

The next morning, I had a dream I was riding the tube in London and they had free dirty apartments everywhere; but the people were very kind. Ryan's angels were playing the trumpet in his room while I am writing this book this morning; breathtakingly beautiful.

Beautiful day and trail rode my horses tonight. Ryan being silly shared with me that the archangels are preparing him for a battle with the devil. Faith in Archangel Michael, Ryan is a chosen one.

I stayed up late making a video out of the east wing by the dock the next morning as I watched it, it was God and all of the archangels. This is their angel portal at Eagle Point and that is Behind the Veil.

I had unrest and sadness the Saturday before Palm Sunday, I tried to cheer up Ryan with a new mattress to get rid of the smell of the haunting in his room last year and Zeus came down with laminitis again.

It is Palm Sunday and it has a special sadness in it. Ryan and I both have a very strong love of Jesus Christ and there's also a strange tension in the house and grounds. I worked on the book and videoed Gods star, there were thousands and thousands of angels; just magical. Quiet night, just a very strange tension and vibration.

I spent some quiet time the next day reflecting over the events of the last year and went over all of the pictures and videos I took of the angels. Jesus Christ, divine love, has healed this home and grounds. Faith, grace and gratitude.

And the fun was yet to come, Ryan and I were in for a very special Easter this year; the best one I've ever had in my life.

This year, there are fields of beautiful white flowers, purple violas, pink lilies and yellow flowers covering the entire farm, as if we were in our own heavenly spiritual realm here and we are. My divine grace and gratitude to Mother Mary, Mary Magdalene and Mother Earth.

We were in for a big winter storm tonight with a tornado warning at 2 am. Ryan and I slept right through it, not even realizing that we had had a power outage.

The next morning was so surreal, as of waking up in heaven, sensing Jesus Christ's magical essence. He had left another white angel feather on my kitchen table.

I went and took Ryan to the school bus today and the grounds had a very high vibration. We made it halfway down their driveway and I realized we lost six 100-year-old trees that were downed across the driveway and it just hit me, *Wow, we had another tornado.* Ryan ran to the bus and my guardian angel helped me going in reverse my car over half a mile. I turned to go to the stable to give Zeus his medication and breakfast and I noticed a 100-year-old cedar tree fell on the pasture in between the pump house and my stable and I lost several hundred feet of down pasture board fence on three sides of my pasture.

I was granted another miracle, Zeus was 100% sound today when he couldn't even stand up yesterday and you can feel the presence of our heavenly father, Almighty God, Jesus Christ and all of the archangels here today in our home with me.

With me and Ryan asleep, and my horses asleep in their stable in their stalls last night, we had been protected over two tornadoes through the property that would have caused certain death: me, Ryan and my horses. God has control over the weather and that's what the strange tension from Palm Sunday was about.

The next morning, God shined his light on me, the same symbol Ryan showed me in the pictures, divine diamond crystal light shining on the Cove this morning as close to heaven on Earth as you can get.

Ryan would tell me today when he got home from school that God asked him to tell me not to take any more videos or pictures of him or his angel's portals. My face turned beet red completely embarrassed, I agreed. Who wouldn't want to look at pictures and videos of angels and

God I was seeing things here at Eagle Point which were an honor that no one else on Earth have the pleasure of.

As I thought about it, I understood why; Eagle Point was a protected place Jesus Christ and the archangels to channel and visit with Ryan and it only takes one Satan worshiper to conjure up another haunting. Beautiful, peaceful night.

The next day, my guardian angel and what must have been many more angels with me, lent me warrior strength to somehow mend all those fences in my horses' pasture by myself, so I could turn my horses out. I absolutely do not know how I did it.

Later that day, I was guided to do some research on the BC era dates and found that Jesus Christ's true birthday was March twenty-third the same as Ryan's. I couldn't wait to tell Ryan we when he got out of speech therapy class and when he did, I said, "Ryan, you and Jesus have the same birthday."

He replied, "I already know; he told me. And it must remain a secret."

I just laughed; Ryan was so silly that night, wanting to learn how to hypnotize people, he told me he talks to all of the spirits in the house and they love me and despise Stewart.

I had a beautiful moonlight ride that night, I have so much unconditional love from Ryan and my horses. Tonight, full of joy and surreal peace.

The next morning, I can feel God's presence on my back porch, I heard him tell my guardian angel, "ne hath spoken." My horses are also loved by God, I feel like my body has been healed self-love.

The next morning, I saw the blue amoeba spirit I love to watch slide onto the cove next to the pool where the extraterrestrial UFO had crash-landed and Ryan and I giggled. Archangel Metatron was there.

We had a major lightning storm that night and when I was on my back porch, before I went to bed, the lightning bolt narrowly missed the house. Thank you again, God, for your protection.

Ryan communicates with this blue amoeba spirit and Ryan says it loves me. Easter weekend festivities, the archangels were in and out of Ryan's room all day long and Ryan and Archangel Metatron satisfied my curiosity about this blue amoeba spirit I've seen sliding around and the neighbor and I's cove. Ryan told me projecting Archangel Metatron's voice, "It is a Viking Seal from Mars."

He then said that the green beacon in the sky on latitude 37 above the cove is a beacon sign of Mars and the orange and blue rays that show up in the pictures with craters on it with silver cords everywhere in the sky is a colony of

Martians just as I suspected. I asked Ryan what do they eat and he replied, "Bugs. They eat bugs."

I laughed hysterically. Ryan told me they are hundreds of thousands of Martians from Mars above the cove in a colony and also a colony underground. I asked him if they abduct human beings and perform experiments on them and he replied yes and shivered; he was not fond of them.

Now I know why our cricket population has been depleted, the blue amoeba Viking Seal from Mars slides around the land off the coves, collecting bugs for food. I also understand now how very protective that cove is from natural disaster. Ryan was with God tonight, immense joy and harmony; angels everywhere.

Heavenly Easter sunrise, angels all over the house and the archangels in and out of Ryan's room all day. I spent the whole day preparing a feast in honor of Jesus Christ. I baked a cross cake with purple glitter with fresh flowers decorating it from the yard and Easter lilies on the dining room table with handmade cross.

I was in the front yard and Ryan asked, out of the blue, where the gold bullion was. I thought to myself, *His angels must have overheard me tell my girlfriend Alice the story of the sunken pirate ship in the cove with gold treasure.*

A photo of the pirate ship had shown up in a picture when Archangel Michael's angels of legions were here clearing the house last year.

I was supposed to be shown this ship in the picture. I giggled; I could sense Archangel Metatron's presence and how much fun Ryan has with God.

I showed him the area of the cove and where the pirate ship had sunk and told him what Archangel Michael had shown me.

We had a very special dinner. Ryan wore a dress shirt and tie. His angels blessed our meal and we said a special prayer of divine grace to Jesus Christ, full of love, harmony and rejoice.

The next day, when I picked Ryan up from the school bus, I asked him if God had sent mermaids to the sunken pirate ship to find the gold bullion and he replied, "Yes, they found it." I was very pleased, the gold bullion belongs in heaven.

My horses are unicorns, my own fairy tale. They have hearts of gold. I would be tested through dreams the next few days, as my old self would metaphorically be gone and my new soul would be pure with faith to Jesus Christ.

The first one, I was being judged at court and I had a black cat with me. The judge fell in love with me and my feminine intimacy. I enjoyed his aura, he wanted to be sexual with me, and the angels showed me he was married so I turned him down. No shame, every woman likes to feel desirable.

The next one, a very tall African American woman appeared with a large afro, she had been in my dreams several other times. For some reason, she showed up in the restroom of a nice restaurant I was having dinner at. I looked at her and had a warning bell go off, she tried to hand me a napkin to dry my hands. She had piercing black eyes. I looked down at her hands and she had extremely long devil-shaped black fingernails. I smiled and walked away, not accepting the napkin. I thought about this dream a lot when I woke up and I thank you once again Archangel Michael for cutting yet another ethereal attachment from the dark side that was in my soul. I felt enormously better after this one.

That afternoon, I was putting the laundry away in my bedroom while Ryan was in the kitchen playing with his angels and I heard a little girl crying in the hallway. I went to look and I saw Eva, my psychic cat, staring at what I thought had to be a ghost. I could hear her but could not see her. I went and fetched Ryan and ask him if he saw the little girl ghost and he said, "Yes, I do." I asked him to call Archangel Michael to release her she wanted to go to heaven with her mother and Ryan closed his eyes and did. I heard his angels say, "Your mom sure can hear!"

1:11 11:11 Ryan hand I have so much fun at Eagle Point I adore him. I was reminded again that evening from God's messenger that this house and land has been abused and raked through the coals for hundreds of years by Indians, Brits, French, Norse, Pirates, Yankees and carpetbaggers. It was a magnet for demons and ghosts. Ryan and I, God,

Jesus Christ and the archangels are the first love this land has ever had in hundreds of years; rejoice in Jesus Christ.

I fantasized that night about buying a castle, a French Chateau in France, taking Ashley, Ryan, my horses and birds to France and explore Europe and Mary Magdalene land.

Ironically, the next morning Ryan told me we needed to move to another country. He also shared with me he can see into the future.

That night, there was something lurking around the back porch, I dreamt about my frustration with Stewart not putting any time, effort or money into Eagle Point or into our almost nonexistent relationship. God will work on this for me.

I woke up the next morning annoyed that my body was sore and cold. After I said my meditation prayers in the stable, I heard four very loud sonic booms above the cove and alien vibration sound.

I heard Archangel Michael land above the dormer of the kitchen and then he landed above the stable. No fear. He healed the pain in my body and asked why I was not communicating with Maryanne the psychic anymore and I told him she had cut her cords being afraid of abduction from aliens. I love Archangel Michael's vibration.

I had a nice lunch with my friend Alice today, her husband is a famous ex-Super Bowl star and I asked Ryan when he got home from school what had happened at the house today and he told me Archangel Michael was just visiting.

I asked Ryan if he was here during his visit even though he was at school and he shyly confessed that he can be at multiple locations at the same time, just like the archangels.

The next morning, I had a very prolific dream as I always do after being in Archangel Michael's presence. My dream I had an ethereal attachment from my childhood who was a murderer and liked to slit people's throats and then I dreamt about the crazy path my mom had given me and my brother throughout my childhood. Thank you, Archangel Michael, once again.

Ryan worked at Walter Reed Hospital today and said he really enjoyed it. I'm not surprised he enjoys being with healers and empathetic people.

That night, Ryan rode his bike to the mailbox and came back upset saying that God had deceived him by promising him to go to college. I counseled Ryan he was being tested and lured by a demon.

We talked about faith and patience and divine timing and I reminded him Jesus Christ spent 40 days in the wilderness tested by God. I told him how much God and Jesus Christ love him; they are his family. He announced he was going to speak with God tonight. I smiled and went for a moonlight trail ride.

The next morning, Ryan was humbled and said he felt much better, we were filled with peace and harmony today. As I was going about my day, my guardian angel spoke to me and told me that the devil had hidden cords in these grounds and how sneaky demons are. They even disguise themselves as angels to lure you in.

I had a pleasant day and that afternoon, when I went upstairs to take a bath, I heard Archangel Michael land on the attic. I always know his presence is coming as I bow, curtsy, twirl and dance as I just had done in the dining room and hallway on my way upstairs.

After I got dressed, I went into the kitchen to work on my book and at approximately 2:22, I heard Archangel Michael land on the kitchen dormer with more force than I had ever heard before.

The windows were shaking and the doors rattled, I thought the roof was going to cave in. This lasted for about 5 minutes; I looked out the window and all the squirrels that live in the trees next to the kitchen were running away from the house, terrified; as were the birds. I thought for a split-second about taking a picture, then absolutely not, as Archangel Michael battles demons, this must have been Satan and who would ever want to look at one. There was absolutely no fear on my part. I thank you once again archangel Michael. Faith, joy, peace, divine love grace and gratitude to Jesus Christ. It was quiet for the rest of the day.

Ryan was in a very intense conversation with his angels tonight. I could hear them instructing and teaching him but let them have their privacy. Ryan would be working with Archangel Michael and Archangel Metatron the next few days, scouting the grounds.

Angel feathers and feathers from my spirit guides today. Ryan and I had a great time at the Saint Therese Church luncheon for the Bread for Life Food Pantry volunteers. We sat with the pastor and executive director; I felt accepted there, new beginnings that will be our home Church.

We had a blessed day with beautiful birds, six baby Canadian goslings, and Ryan has been visiting God every single night and having very intense conversations with His angels, they also have fun too. We had a magical sunset that night with pure, golden flames filled with love from God.

The next morning, I was prompted to explore the house all day looking for secret, hidden compartments in the walls containing documents and secret treasures. The walls here are brick lath and plaster and someone else had already chiseled away at the fireplaces looking for secret treasure. There were copperhead snake skins in the holes in the walls; the walls are filled here with snakes.

A psychic friend of mine told me that there was a trapped soul in the boiler room in the basement and a glass jar filled with a hex and an evil cord underground my stable.

God's golden Rays shining tonight I asked Ryan to ask Archangel Michael and Archangel Metatron to send dozens of fairies into the walls of the house, the boiler room and the stable to find the secret treasure and remove the hex. That night my spirit guides sent me a toad in the stable. Toad is the symbol of an opportunity to contact your most primal, instinctual self that is the seed of spiritual growth...

I had a beautiful ride tonight and Ryan and I have so much fun together in this magical place; then that night, I heard army of UFOs coming in and then I was blessed with watching the fairies and the angels combing every inch of the grounds and the house. You could see thousands of violet and green fairies and hundreds of angels all over the front yard and fields and everywhere in the house.

The next night, I was blessed with a visit from God in my kitchen, there were diamond-like triangles shining all over the walls and the floor. Pure joy. They had found the secret treasures and documents in the house.

The next morning was Mother's Day, and, in my dreams Archangel Michael took me white water rafting with the grizzly bears in the rivers in heaven, it was breathtaking pristinely beautiful and so amazing, magical, and fun, I asked Ryan when I took him to school if he went white water rafting with Archangel Michael this morning and he replied, "Yes, I did," with a big smile. This was my Mother's Day blessing from God. Thank you.

Interestingly today, we had a black heron in the pond, I have never seen one before; I researched them, they are from Africa. Nothing would surprise me at Eagle Point.

The next morning, I had a very prolific dream from God that it is his will to turn this book into a movie and he requested a beautiful redhead with straight hair and bangs, very innocent and very beautiful, to star in the movie.

Very surreal here today, the horses went swimming out to the island; it seems as if time is standing still and I'm enjoying the peace and harmony here.

That afternoon, I was having a rough time with Ryan over his disappointment of not being able to go to college this year. I walked the stress off and went horseback riding when I got back home Ryan shared a YouTube album with me to sing with God, it was Hilltop songs with Jesus Christ; it was also in Tagalog language.

I asked Ryan if he understood Tagalog and he said yes and then I realized he understands all languages like Jesus Christ.

The next morning, we were blessed with the most beautiful sunrise. I was in my special place on the back porch overlooking the cove. God was shining heaven on earth to Eagle Point today, it was like a diamond river dazzling, glistening all over. Absolutely mesmerizing. Then, the water and the triangles turned pink. I watched this magic for a very long time.

I went to the kitchen to make breakfast and looked outside and all of a sudden, all of the green grass turned solid gold.

I decided I really wanted my mother, who is 78, and has cancer to move to Eagle Point to experience the peace and love here until she passes. I would be given a very strong guidance from Jesus Christ on this subject in a few days.

I picked lettuce from my garden today and a lady bug crawled on my hand a sign from Mother Mary's protection, I can feel her love around me. I had to lit a Mother Mary candle in my room in honor of her this morning.

I made a wish from the ladybug. I first thought I wanted to be a psychic like Ryan, then changed my mind; I wanted Ashley and Ryan to have happy, fulfilling lives and be successful; that's what Mother Mary would want.

I made time for solitude today enjoying the silence meditating in Mother Nature, something I thought was lost in my life would be returning; that would be my intuition, my mother, self-love, spirituality and my relationship with Jesus Christ.

Today, there was sonic booming up Behind the Veil in the cove. That night was so silly; there were herds of elephants running through the house and Archangel Michael and Archangel Metatron.

This was a message from Jesus Christ. My integral service in life shall be to service my children and my mother and do not let anything stand in the way of this at all cost. Trust senses and smells, loyalty and connect with a divine and so it is.

The next morning, we were blessed with another absolutely magical sunrise, brilliant diamond triangles radiating on the cove that turned violet and Archangel Raphael was shining his green healing light through my soul, then the diamonds turned gold and then pink. Archangel Gabriel and Archangel Ariel, divine love.

This gave me an overwhelming sense of peace, joy, and love from God, our Heavenly Father, Jesus Christ, the archangels and all of God's angels.

And when Jesus Christ makes his second coming, Zeus and Coconut are going to wear elaborate headdresses on their heads, with feathers jewels made of gold, and white roses braided in their manes and tails, and pull a golden chariot with Jesus Christ and his angels to town. And tonight, we have archangel Uriel here and Ryan is in a heated meeting up in his room with His angels.

The next morning, God's angels helped me in the stable while my horses were having their hooves trimmed and Archangel Uriel was present.

Ryan is at peace today and we talked about extraterrestrials in the car. He advised me that in the year

2105, they will be coexisting with human beings on Earth; I just laughed. After the horseshoer left Zeus, injured his left-hand foot and could not stand up, he's in absolute agony.

The next day, was uneventful and then Sunday came. We went to Mass. Father Gregory had a beautiful white aura around him today and then he announced that Jesus Christ was with us in church and I felt a pang of overwhelming sadness about crucifixion. I invited Father Gregory to have dinner with us and God's angels.

Zeus is still lame and still an agony 6 days later he still can't stand up even after four grams of bute a day.

July 15th, Jesus Christ performed his third miracle, saving Zeus. My guardian angel told me it was a very, very serious injury and will take a long time for him to fully recover. The devil is so sneaky, preying on people with hearts of gold to cause anguish and is a test of faith. My horseshoer confirmed the next time he came to shoe the horses that Zeus had fractured the tip of his coffin bone and it somehow miraculously healed.

The next morning, we were blessed with Jesus Christ at sunrise, shining his divine white light and love down on me and Ryan. On the 25th, we will have a special feast with Jesus, the archangels and Saints, and it will be a magical one in honor and gratitude of the Lord.

When I went out to ride my horses later that afternoon, I saw a red-eyed demon disguised as a human wearing a black suit and a black hat with a mustache, watching me from the tractor barn.

I told Ryan about this and we would discuss it later. It is amazing what divine timing and synchronicity can do for your life and living in the peace and joy of God's holy harmony. Interesting. Everyone in our house always wakes up at 5:55 am.

Since this time Ashley has moved home which is God's will and Jesus Christ has a very special interest in Ashley and how religion is affecting the millennial group era.

Ashley is very happy here ending her relationship with her ex-boyfriend and adjusting to having freedom and control over her own life.

We had a beautiful family dinner the next night with Stewart, Ashley and Ryan and I with all of His angels present. I went outside on my back porch after dinner and I heard a pack kangaroos jumping on my back porch. My spirit guide showed me our needs will always be met and keep family strength, don't look back and take leaps and bounds.

The next morning, Ryan and I were discussing August 8th and the lions gate portal and crystalline feminine healing from Archangel Raphael for planet Earth.

We had a nice morning with the help of God's beautiful, loving, and protective angels and after a beautiful night ride, Archangel Gabriel visited me and told me the passcode to the lions gate was three-time thrice, he repeated this three times and that it was extremely important that Ryan be present and we all must go through this portal and that Archangel Michael, Archangel Faith, Archangel Metatron and Archangel Raphael will all be with us on August 8th to accomplish going through the portal.

Ryan is a very gifted psychic. He speaks light language which is how he communicates with Holy Spirit, Jesus Christ and all of the archangels, not to mention every being in the universe.

We are experiencing an incredible vibration of peace and joy at Eagle Point in preparation for the lions gate portal and the angels are sharing with me the reason preparation is so crucial in part of the history of this land and then they do silly things like putting 7 blue herons on my porch and five egrets standing next to me and then a herd of dinosaurs in the front yard and I just laugh.

The next morning, August 7th, we had the pinkest most incredible divine sunrise from Archangel Cameel with God shining love and rays of light at us intense joy and peace.

Lions gate day, August 8th, we are blessed with amazing, incredible, love of the presence of God and Jesus and the angels. It's all about gratitude and rejoicing in the light and love of Jesus Christ.

Today, Ryan and I listened to a transmission from Anna Jones a pastor and an angel communicator from Hawaii who was putting a public transmission from Archangel Raphael for lion's gate.

Ryan and I listened to this for several hours and when she transmitted Archangel Raphael and his light language, Ryan shared with me exactly what he was saying. Divine bliss.

Everyone's timing for lion's gate was a day off. On August 9th, I was sitting on my back porch after riding and at 8:54 pm, I saw God, our heavenly father, in the sky shooting solid gold lightning rods from the heavens into the sky above the Veil and the lion appeared and filled his soul up with Holy Spirit, and then the portal opened and we went through the gate and God guided us through the portal.

Archangel Michael and Archangel Uriel stayed with us this night and I saw the diamond crystalline grid from Jesus Christ on the cove is the most beautiful, incredible event I've ever experienced in my life.

One of my friends emailed me a book called *The Law of Oneness*, it was absolutely fascinating about RA, a Holy Spirit communicator filled with extraterrestrials, multi dimensions, and the negativity of the people that inhabit this planet. I asked Ryan later if he talks to RA and he replied yes.

We will be planning a feast in honor of the Divine and Mother Mary next Thursday and it is full moon energy very important.

Archangel Michael is continuing cutting cords and emotions from everyone that lives in this house through dreams and signs from spirit guides.

My relationship with Stewart is pretty much non-existent he rarely ever comes to Eagle Point anymore and this is for my highest good. Stewart does not have any faith or compassion for anyone and is controlled by greed.

The next day Ryan and I went to Walmart and when we were checking out behind us one of the Martians had followed us and tried to disguise himself as a human. I pointed and showed Ryan and we both literally started cracking up, then we went to Aldi's to get some fruit and one of the ghosts tried to get in the car and follow us home and Ryan tried to explain to him that mommy doesn't want ghost in her house. I just laughed. All in a day of a life with a psychic kid.

Ryan would spend most of his time throughout the rest of his summer vacation with the Lord and the archangels in training; his conversations are mostly private and he is very loyal to them. They do share some things with me and it's beautiful to watch the Viking Seals around the cove and God's beautiful angels everywhere.

Jesus is making plans for my mother to come back here and Holy Spirit, Archangel Michael and Archangel Raphael showed themselves to me on the cove and will heal my mother from the demons that are attached to her and her health so she can live the rest of her life in peace with her family.

That evening, my daughter and I were sitting on my back porch talking about life and the future and out of nowhere the archangels and God blessed us with the most beautiful golden lightning show and beautiful lightning rods of blue and green and fuchsia and violet and rainbow colors coming out from the heavens on the cove.

Ashley and I really enjoyed being blessed by this beautiful moment.

Most people think of Jesus Christ and honor his crucifixion in selfishness for their own glory wanting instant miracles, abundance of money and wealth.

Every time I think of Jesus Christ, I think of him in all of his glory and gratitude in the highest and have the utmost divine gratitude and love for blessing us with his peace and joy, holy harmony and God's angels.

Ryan and I joined as patrons at St. Therese Catholic Church and the Lord has given me abundance of time to continue to volunteer at the food bank and feed the poor.

Ryan is in the living room in a heated conversation with Jonathan Bryant's spirit about the events that happened at Eagle Point Plantation hundreds of years ago. Ryan told me that Jonathan respected me for being brave enough to live here and was happy that I was saved by the Lord and he felt very sorry for me for the way Stewart treated me. I was listening to their conversation from the hallway and smiled to myself as Jonathan has been deceased for over three hundred years.

Today is September 6th, the day hurricane Dorian is hammering the East Coast and thank you to the Lord for sparing us from harm and in the utmost irony, the email from your publishing company was sent to me on September 3rd, my 52nd birthday with a contract to publish Behind the Veil. God works in mysterious ways.

And I am sure there will be several sequels to this book as every day at Eagle Point Plantation is a new experience.

And as a closing to this chapter of my life I am listening to God's angels playing the trumpet, harp and flute to the most incredible holy presentation to the Lord's ears as Ryan is channeling upstairs in his room to God at approximately 11:11.

Glory to God and peace and goodwill to those that follow him.